Gentle Rhythm

Touch the Sea Series, Volume 2

Autumn Gaze

Published by Dark Shadow Publishing, 2022.

GENTLE RHYTHM

First edition. December 7, 2022.

Written by Autumn Gaze.

Also by Autumn Gaze

Department of Defense Series
Dead Ahead
Blue Falcon
Joint Service
Indirect Attack

Touch the Sea Series
Seduction Island
Gentle Rhythm

Wicked Fates Series
Beautiful Darkness
Twisted Darkness
Wicked Darkness

Watch for more at www.autumngaze.com.

Copyright 2022 By Autumn Gaze

TOUCH THE SEA BOOK TWO
Gentle
rhythm
bestselling author
autumn gaze

Gentle Rhythm Blurb

I will find comfort in the rhythm of the sea...

Ethan Mitchell and Ava Hunt are through. She thinks he's a jerk, and he knows he has to stay away from Ava or risk his family's scandal growing even larger.

Though neither wants to admit it, they can't stop thinking about each other. When Ethan is discovered by the media he's been hiding from, the only one there to help is Ava. Despite her misgivings, she gives in and lets him hide out at her apartment.

Can they outlast the reporters, or will their still-burning desire for one another win out?

Touch the Sea Series

Book 1 – Seduction Island
Book 2 – Gentle Rhythm
Book 3 – Dancing on Waves
Book 4 – Stormy Waters
Book 5 – Tempting the Ocean

Find Autumn Gaze:

Autumn Gaze Newsletter:
https://www.autumngaze.com/sign-up
Autumn Gaze Facebook Page:
https://www.facebook.com/AutumnGazeAuthor
Autumn Gaze Website:
http://www.autumngaze.com

Want to read more...
For **FREE?**
Sign up for Autumn's newsletter
And she'll send you updates on new releases, ARC copies of books
and a whole lotta fun!
Sign up for news and updates!
https://www.autumngaze.com/sign-up[1]

---

1. https://l.facebook.com/l.php?u=https%3A%2F%2Fwww.autumngaze.com%2Fsign-up%3Ffb-clid%3DIwAR19Pln3ibiSJ3sbPjqwZi2C2ouEk0HNj3WPfqfFHOACbgTxP-nyPseA8z2I&h=AT2zXnGSz1iKPMdJCv3D1jaSfPpsk9GF78_lcDB8lQuthwcLpds-du_0dX1lpDVC_R_aw9eie2R8y7wQzGrIpKgoi-6TEh8H8t1IcDKGEJ-NzgaLtedWWgkAd-PDYhWUrxkU

TOUCH THE SEA BOOK TWO
Gentle
rhythm
bestselling author
autumn gaze

Chapter One

Ava

"No, no, no," I groaned and tossed the blouse on the bed.

I didn't know why I was giving my outfit so much energy. I wasn't that excited for the date. I was only going because I felt like it was the only way to get over Ethan. I doubted it would work, but I was doing it anyway. I refused to sit around and sulk. It felt like I was letting him win if I did. The date was with some Navy guy—Chris. I didn't even know his last name. I didn't care to know. I doubted the date was going to go anywhere. My goal was to prove to myself I could go out with another man.

I wanted the date to go well, but I didn't. Ethan had burned me. He made me feel like shit. Like a damn fool for letting myself get involved with him at all. I knew I should always trust my gut. When the next wealthy New York man showed up at my door again, I would know better.

Stumped and unable to find something to wear, I called Andrea on video chat. "I need help," I said when she picked up.

She was on the treadmill. "What kind of help?" she asked breathlessly.

"I need help picking out what to wear tonight," I said. "I want something pretty but not sexy."

"Is it the Navy boy tonight?" she asked.

"Yes."

"Hold on," she said and jumped off the treadmill. She took a drink of water and wiped her face. "Okay, what are we working with?" she asked.

I flipped the phone around to show her the blouses I had tossed on the bed.

"I like the red," I heard her say.

I turned the phone around with my nose wrinkled. "I don't know." I sighed. "It seems a little extra."

"It's perfect," she said. "You're just trying to find an excuse not to go on the date. You need to go. This is the best way to put stinky, old Ethan in your rearview mirror."

I wouldn't call him stinky, but I understood what she meant. "I know I'm not going to be great company. It's going to end up being a shitty date."

"Hmm, if I remember correctly, there was this woman who used to tell me to choose happiness," she teased.

"I know, I know," I groaned. "Between Ethan and Jenny, I swear I'm going to lose my mind. My life was so easy until they both showed up."

"Have you talked to Jenny again?" she asked.

"Nope," I said with a shake of my head. "I don't know what she expects me to do. She gets herself into these messes all the time. I don't know why she thinks I should do anything to help her. How could I possibly help her? I don't even know what she did. I don't want to know."

"She's your sister," Andrea reminded me.

"Not really," I said. "She hasn't been my sister in a few years. She chose that life. She didn't want anything to do with me when I needed her most. Jenny is all about searching for the next sugar daddy. She wants to make sure she marries rich."

"She didn't even give you a hint about what might be wrong?" she asked.

"Nope," I answered. "Just said it was bad."

"Weird," she said and took another drink. "I take it you haven't heard from Ethan again?"

"No," I said.

"You sound pissed."

"I'm not pissed, but it is kind of messed up that he didn't try a little harder to apologize," I said. "I thought maybe he would send flowers or something. He just went crazy and says 'oops.' Like that's going to make it better. He accused me of stealing. That's messed up. He could have accused me of doing just about anything. But stealing and selling his secrets? That's low. That was rude and obnoxious. It was arrogant. I have never felt like such shit."

"I'm sorry," she said. "It really was not cool."

I pushed away the thoughts that had been weighing on me and making me feel bad. Ethan's betrayal had hit hard. His unfounded accusations hurt. I didn't know how or why he thought I would ever steal anything from him. We had a beautiful night together and I let myself think there was a real chance we might actually be able to have a relationship. He proved I was right about him from the very beginning. He was nothing but a jerk.

"Thanks," I said. "I better go and get dressed for this date."

"You sound so happy about it." She laughed.

"I'm only doing this because you think I should," I told her. "And because I'm really hoping he will somehow make me forget all about that asshole."

"It might take a couple of times, but you'll get there," she promised. "I'm sorry he was a pig and I'm sorry I encouraged you to go for it. Unfortunately, there are always a few bad apples in the bunch. If there was a quick and easy way to weed them out, life would be too easy. It's part of the game. We have to try out a lot until we find the right one."

"That sounds very philosophical." I laughed. "Since when did you get so wise?"

"I'm telling you, that trip changed me. I feel clearer and brighter. I see the world differently. I was even thinking about getting a job."

I feigned a heart attack. "No! Not a job!"

"Stop," she said, laughing. "Not like your kind of job, but there's the chance I might get to work with kids at a developmental center. It's just a few hours a week teaching art, but it might be fun."

"You should do it," I said. "Put that art degree to good use. I think you're going to find it's very rewarding."

"We'll see," she replied. "I don't want to get too carried away. My parents might think I'm trying to be a grown up and independent, and cut me off."

"Oh, the horror," I teased.

"That's what I said." She grinned.

"For real, Andrea. That's awesome. I think you're going to love it. I'm proud of you."

"Thank you," she said, and I could see the excitement in her eyes. "Call me tomorrow and let me know how it went."

"I will," I said and ended the chat.

I was proud of her for trying to do something with her life. She didn't have to work. She could continue to live off family money and do nothing. I was glad she was changing her ways. I put my phone down and got dressed with no enthusiasm. The last date I had been on had ended badly. Technically, the date had been great, but then he turned into a total asshole.

I was pissed. Hurt. And just feeling like a damn fool. I really thought Ethan would have called me. Yes, he called, but only a few times. Then he just stopped. He gave up. That told me he didn't really care. He might have felt bad for a minute, but he was quickly over it. I wasn't surprised. He was going to go back to his life in New York and that would be that. I was just the dumbass that fell for the guy after having sex a couple of times.

I pushed Ethan to the back of my mind where he belonged. I didn't want to waste even another second thinking about him. He wasn't worth it. I would forget about him as soon as there was something else, rather someone else, to focus my attention on. Once Ethan was gone, I could start working on the house again. I wanted to do some renovating in the guest bathroom. That would help occupy my time. I needed a project. Maybe I could buy another house. A real shithole that would require me to work around the clock. I wouldn't have time to eat, think, or even sleep.

That's what I would do. I was going to scour the foreclosures and find a new project. Tomorrow. Today, I had to go on a date with Chris. I had to try. I dressed and put on a little makeup. The contradiction between getting ready for this date versus the date with Ethan was pretty stark. I couldn't bring myself to really care about what whether or not he was impressed by me.

I met Chris at the restaurant. I didn't want him knowing where I lived just yet. Chris was dressed in a Hawaiian shirt and khakis. It wasn't really my favorite look, but it was pretty common.

"Hi." He smiled nervously and kissed my cheek.

I took my seat at the table. It was one of the touristy restaurants that served barbecue. Not my favorite, but again, it was standard fare. "Did you work today?" I asked conversationally.

"This morning." He nodded.

He was a handsome guy. Young and full of life. He reminded me of a young Brad Pitt. He had blond hair and blue eyes with a very boyish, country boy look. His smile was what convinced me to agree to go out with him. He was a nice guy. I was thinking a nice guy was exactly what I needed after Ethan. I let myself be swayed by the edgy, cocky thing. That blew up in my face.

"How long have you been here?" I asked him.

"Just got here last month," he replied. "I was in Japan for a while. I've been trying to get stationed here since I joined the Navy."

"How long have you been in the Navy?" I asked.

"Seven years," he answered.

"Is it your career or do you plan on exiting soon?" I asked.

He shrugged. "I'm not sure. I have another year on my current contract. Do you live here fulltime?"

"I do." I nodded and forced a smile. The small talk was normal. I was just looking for some spark. It wasn't happening. Yet.

"How long have you lived here in Oahu?"

"I lived here when I was little," I said. "My dad was Navy and stationed here for a while. I moved back about five years ago."

"It's beautiful here," he said. "I think I might retire here if I can swing it. The cost of living is pretty steep. I'm not sure what I'll do for work. How do you make it work?"

I laughed. "I work. A lot. I work at the coffee shop and I do dog walking. Sometimes I do some housecleaning. And I have a few rental properties I own."

"Damn," he said with a chuckle. "I'm not sure I'm going to make it. You must work around the clock."

"I do work a lot, but it's worth it to live in paradise."

"I get that," he said. "I haven't had a lot of time to really explore, but some of my buddies have told me where to go and what to see."

"Where are you from?" I asked while sipping the fruity cocktail I ordered. I was trying to keep the conversation flowing while controlling it. I didn't want to get personal. I knew I was tanking the potential for a relationship, but I wasn't ready. I was out but holding myself at arm's length.

"Iowa." He grinned.

"Ah, farm boy," I teased.

"Born and raised." He nodded. "My grandparents have a cattle ranch and my parents grow corn and hay."

"You really are a farm boy," I commented.

"I am," he replied. "I had never seen the ocean before I joined the Navy."

"That had to have been a big surprise," I said.

"The best," he replied. "I was in love. I was free."

"Do your parents want you back in Iowa once you're out of the Navy?" I asked.

He flashed a grin. "You know it."

He was a good guy. A guy I should want to be with. But he just wasn't doing it for me. There was no excitement. No layers to find out who the man was underneath a tough exterior. No mystery.

Chapter Two

Ethan

I groaned and leaned back in the chair, my eyes going to the ceiling. Hawaii wasn't far enough from New York. I longed for the days of no cell phones. There was a downside to always being accessible. It meant you could never really get away from the world unless you went somewhere remote enough to claim no service. It was my own fault. I knew what I needed to do. I was the one who couldn't cut the cord.

"No," I murmured in response to one of my father's questions.

He wasn't really looking for a response. He was lecturing me about my lack of participation in the family drama. I didn't see how I needed to be involved. I didn't own a time machine. I couldn't go back in time and keep my brother from buying drags or his friend from dying. Collin fucked up. Period. I couldn't stop that. My only job was to try and manage the damage to the company with the family name. The fallout from the scandal was hitting the company hard. I was trying to keep investors calm while holding onto my job.

With the way things were going, I was going to be lucky to keep my position as CEO of Mitchell Industries. The board was antsy. They wanted to cut ties with me and the family, while holding onto our name. From everything I was hearing, there was a damn good chance it would happen. I was struggling to give a shit about losing my job. I was envisioning a future on a deserted island. The more my dad talked, the more I wanted to run away.

"I've got to go," I said and cut off my dad.

"Ethan!"

I ended the call and dropped my phone on the couch. I felt like I had been through a boxing match. My ears actually hurt. I had spent the last several days on the phone. My dad was pissed at me because I wasn't in New York or hiding out in the Hamptons with them. He seemed to have this idea I could wave a magic wand and make it all go away if I was in New York. I wasn't there. I wasn't going to be able to fix the mess. It was on my brother.

Then I had my mother, who was extremely emotional. She was crushed but for very different reasons than my father. She was sad and wanted me to be there as emotional support. The last thing I wanted to do was spend my days listening to my parents complaining about my brother. Then there was Lucas. He was the voice of reason, but he was also trying to keep the company afloat while running interference for me with the board. I hated that my friend was put into the situation. Everyone except Collin was being raked over the coals. My younger brother was going to skate again. Hundreds of lives were going to be impacted by his choices and he didn't seem to get it.

I loved my brother, but the guy was on the wrong path. He was going down a dark hole and I wasn't sure we were going to be able to pull him back from the disaster. I didn't know how to help Collin. I wasn't sure there was anything to do except let him fall on his face. I supposed I felt a little guilty for letting it get to this point. We all failed him. He had been my sidekick when we were younger. It was him and me against the world.

What happened?

"Collin, come on," I whispered. "They're coming."

My little brother crawled across the floor as if my parents' guests roaming below in the massive foyer wouldn't see him. I was twelve and convinced I was smarter than all the adults in the house. And I fancied myself a spy.

"This way," I hissed and motioned for him to follow me to the service stairs.

We rushed down the dark stairwell and rushed around the back hallway that the housekeepers and service staff used. Collin pushed open the door into the ballroom. Servers were moving around the room and getting things set up for the party. Our parents were always hosting parties. I didn't even know what they were celebrating.

"In here," I said to Collin and pulled back the heavy black curtains that covered one of the huge windows that lined one side of the room. The curtains were usually opened. Collin and I liked to hide in the curtains and eavesdrop on the people my parents were entertaining.

We giggled and snickered when people walked by the curtain without seeing us. "Let's go get a snack," Collin said.

"Wait," I said and grabbed his sleeve. A waiter walked by. "Okay, now go."

We scurried to the back of the room and slipped through the door once again. We made it into the kitchen. The catering staff was rushing around and didn't seem to notice us. Trays were lined up on one counter. I grabbed a few of the sandwich-looking things and handed them off to Collin before going back for more.

"Hey!" One of the staff saw us and shooed us out of the kitchen. We laughed and raced back upstairs to enjoy our stolen treats. We were supposed to stay out of the way when the parties were thrown.

I smiled at the memory. Those were the good days. Our parents were not the most attentive. Their image was very important to them. Parties were the normal thing in the house. Collin and I had to rely on each other. If it wasn't for him, I would have had many lonely days and nights while our parents were doing their thing. I always tried to look out for him.

That brought up a sour feeling. Did I fail him? I had tried so hard to protect him, but when I turned eighteen, I joined the Navy and left Collin alone in that house. He was thirteen at the time. Just starting into the world of being a teenager and going through all that hard stuff—alone. It wasn't long after I left that he started getting into trouble. I tried to call him when I was away, but maybe I didn't call enough. And then there was the first time he got into trouble. Just thinking of that moment brought goosebumps to my body.

"Ethan, it's your father," he said when I answered the phone.

I rolled over to check the time. It was two o'clock in the morning. I had to report to work in two hours. "Dad?" I asked with confusion.

"We need your help," he said.

I was in Florida. I wasn't sure how I was going to help anything when they were in New York. "What's wrong?" I asked.

"It's Collin," he replied.

That woke me up. "What happened?"

"He..." He paused, and I was certain I heard him choking up.

My worst fears were coming to life. Collin had gotten into trouble a year earlier. Ever since, it had been nonstop. He got into drugs, been kicked out of the exclusive school he'd been in, and been in and out of the juvenile court system. The kid had gone off the rails. I had been gone two years. In two years, he had changed from my fun little brother to an angry drug addict.

"Dad?" I asked and sat up. I was imagining the worst.

"Collin overdosed, tonight."

My heart dropped. Tears burned the back of my eyes. "Is he—"

"He's fine. Not fine, but he's alive. Your mother found him and called an ambulance. They were able to revive him, but it was close."

"Shit," I muttered. I didn't know what to say. I'd gone from dead asleep to grief-stricken to stunned in a matter of ten seconds.

"I know you're locked in, but we need you to talk to him," he said. "He's in the hospital and will remain for another day. We want him to go to rehab, but he's refusing."

"He's a minor, make him go," I said angrily. "He has to know he's going to die."

"He won't listen," Dad said. "Your mother is a wreck. Collin has only ever listened to you."

I rubbed a hand over my face. "I can call him tonight."

"We need you home," he said.

"Dad, I'm in the Navy," I reminded him. "I can't just call in sick."

"Take leave," he ordered. "I told you this was a bad idea. Family first."

"He's your son," I reminded him. "Why do I have to parent him?"

"You molded that kid to think you were a superhero," he shot back. "When you left, he stopped listening to us."

I didn't think he had ever listened, but whatever. "I'll see what I can do, but Uncle Sam is more powerful than you or the family name."

"Figure something out!" he barked. "We need you."

That had been the beginning of the end of my relationship with my brother. It had changed that day. I did get leave and I was able to see him. Collin had been forced into rehab. Over the last fifteen years, he had struggled with drugs. He got clean and then he'd go out to a party and score again. Being wealthy gave him connections and protection. People protected him from the fallout of his choices. No one was going to rat him out. No one was holding him accountable.

His choices had ruined our relationship. We were barely on speaking terms. While he was partying, I was working. Collin thrived on risk. I thrived on a good business deal. We all thought he would grow out of it eventually. When he showed an interest in politics, I really thought we were through the worst of it. I had been so wrong. It only got worse. I had been pissed at Collin for a long time because he lived his life without rules.

Now, I was beginning to think he might have had the right idea. Collin would never be accused of not living life to the fullest. He shunned the idea of working in the family business. He might not have been too far off base. I was torn between wanting to fight for my position in the company to hoping I would get fired. I just wasn't sure it was worth it anymore.

All I wanted was Ava. I wanted to pretend I wasn't one of the Mitchells she hated. I wanted us to go back to the night before I accused her of stealing my stupid laptop. I wanted to spend time with her again. I hated the fact she hated me. Even apologizing to Ava wasn't an option. I couldn't drag her into this mess. I had to keep distance between us to protect her. I knew it was only matter of time until someone recognized me. I had to lessen the damage as much as possible.

Chapter Three

Ava

I drove to the restaurant on the beach. It was super trendy with a tiki vibe. I had been to the place many times. It was good, but it attracted a lot of tourists. I probably sounded like a snob, but I had quickly become one of the locals who preferred to hide away.

"You look beautiful," Chris greeted me at the door.

"Thank you." I smiled.

"We have a table waiting," he said.

"Great!"

We were seated at one of the tables on the beach. Sand was our floor. An umbrella over the table was tilted back to give us an obstructed view of the sunset. We ordered drinks and appetizers. It was our second date. I wasn't foolish enough to think he wasn't expecting a little something. I had managed to avoid a kiss the first date. He probably thought I was playing hard to get. I wasn't. I just didn't know if I wanted to take it the next step. There would be a third date and more kissing. Eventually, he would expect sex.

"Everything okay?" he asked.

"Yes." I smiled and sipped my drink. "Why?"

"You looked like you were deep in thought," he replied.

"I was just thinking about what I needed to do at one of my properties," I lied.

"I'm pretty handy with a hammer if you need any help," he offered. "My uncle is a handyman. I've done some work with him."

Dammit. He was good guy. I wanted to like him. "I will keep that in mind," I said. "How was work today?"

He groaned. "We had an extra thirty minutes of PT this morning. Someone screwed up and we all got to pay the price. I'm a little sore."

"I'm sorry," I said. "My dad used to tell me about some of the things they had to do."

"Yeah, the rules have changed a little over the last decade but doing three-hundred push-ups is still rough."

"I used to think I wanted to follow my dad's lead and join the military," I said with a laugh. "Then I figured out I don't like to run, and I really hate being told what to do. That pretty much ruined my military career options."

He laughed and nodded. "Yeah, I was a little arrogant when I first joined. It doesn't take them long to snap you out of that behavior."

We talked a little more and ordered our meals. I was only half-listening while he talked about his family back home. I tried like hell to stay focused. But I also knew if I had to force myself to like him, it wasn't really meant to be. I just could not stop thinking about Ethan. The dude had gotten under my skin. If there was a pill I could take to cure me of this awful infatuation, I would absolutely take it.

As Chris talked, I found myself comparing him to Ethan. Chris was warm and funny. Ethan was hard and reserved. Chris was the kind of man who would settle down and want to have a perfect family. He would be loyal and bend over backward to keep his wife happy. Ethan would probably be a difficult man to live with. He was surly at times. I believed he was inclined to be a loner. I didn't know if there would ever be a future there. But I couldn't stop thinking about it. Chris was the kind of man women looked for. The kind of guy parents would be very pleased to marry their daughters off to.

Why couldn't I find the spark? It would be so much easier if I could just fall for him. Ethan would be forgotten, and I could start a new chapter in my life.

Then I remembered I wasn't looking for love. I didn't really want a relationship. I was enjoying my freedom. I didn't need to fall for Chris. I was just trying to find a way to make myself feel less miserable. Chris wasn't a Band-Aid.

"Do you want to go for a walk on the beach?" Chris asked. "I've heard there's a good, shaved ice truck not too far."

"Sure." I forced a smile.

I told myself to get my head straight. I liked shaved ice. I wasn't sure if I would consider it a dessert but whatever. We followed the path down to the beach that looked like a busy park with people and kids enjoying the cool evening. The section of beach was very popular with the tourists. The concession stands were packed.

"It really is something," he said.

"What do you mean?" I asked.

"The beach," he said. "It's stunning. Can you imagine what it would have looked like before the beaches were littered with high-rise hotels?"

"It definitely changed the landscape," I remarked. "I've seen a few pictures of it before it really took off."

"Really?"

"Yes." I smiled. "It was beautiful and natural."

"I'd like to see those pictures," he said.

"Visit some of the smaller restaurants that aren't on the strip," I told him. "Many of them have pictures posted. Some businesses have been around for decades. The history here is exciting. There are plenty of locals who would love to share it."

"You sound very passionate about it," he said.

"I am." I nodded.

"Was your dad native to Hawaii?" he asked.

"No." I laughed. "He was born and raised in New Jersey."

"What about your mom?"

"New York through and through." I smiled.

"I would have never guessed," he said. "You seem like you were born to be here."

"I think I was," I replied. "It's why I'll never leave."

That seemed to give him pause. "Really? You want to spend the rest of your life here?"

"I do."

"But doesn't it get old after a while?" he asked. "It's beautiful, yes, but it's kind of small. What if you want to take a road trip or go somewhere that isn't tropical?"

"You mean the mountains?" I asked.

"Yes."

I pointed to one of the peaks. "Right there."

He laughed and bumped his hip against mine. "I mean the mountains with snow and pine trees. What if you want to go skiing?"

"If I wanted to do that, then I would buy a plane ticket to somewhere there was skiing, just like people who live on the mainland do," I replied.

"What about an escape to the country?" he asked.

"You mean cornfields?" I joked.

"Yeah, something like that." He nodded. "A long drive on a dirt road with nothing but land in front of you. A good road trip that takes you a thousand miles away from your starting point. You can't do that here."

"I think anywhere you live is going to have some perks," I said. "Can you walk out of your cornfield and onto a sandy beach? Can you wear shorts and flipflops in January? Are you surrounded by lush mountains with hundreds of secluded waterfalls just waiting to be discovered?"

He started laughing. "Touché."

"I thought you said you liked it here and were considering making it your permanent home?" I asked.

"I think I like the beauty and the idea, but then I got to thinking about a life here every single day for years," he said. "I guess it made me a little twitchy."

"I think there are going to be upsides and downsides to anywhere you choose to live," I said. "You have to choose what is right for you. Hawaii isn't for everyone. An Iowan farm isn't for everyone."

"Is this where you want to stay forever?" he asked.

It felt like I was at a job interview. Was he interviewing me for the position of his wife? If so, the man was getting way ahead of himself. I told myself not to get irritated by his questions. It was just conversation. He didn't want to waste time dating someone he would never have a future with. I supposed I respected that. I knew he wasn't my future.

"I don't know," I answered. "I think it's a little foolish to try and plan forever when I'm not yet thirty. I might wake up tomorrow and decide I want to live in Alaska. I'm not someone who thinks that hard about my future. I'm more concerned about what happens tomorrow. Are you a planner?"

"I don't know." He shrugged. "Maybe. I know I've got to decide sooner rather than later."

"Because it's time to resign?" I asked.

"I've got an opportunity to pursue a promotion," he said. "I'm not sure I want to stay in. I guess I'm just trying to take a peek into my future. I'm not sure which way to go."

"I think you have to do what feels right to you," I told him. "I don't think Hawaii is going to be where you're happy for the rest of your life. Then again, there isn't a contract you sign in blood if you move here. You are allowed to leave."

He laughed. "Good point. I get in my head sometimes. Sorry. I'm not trying to pressure you."

"It's fine." I smiled. "Sometimes it's nice just to have someone to bounce things off of."

We walked along talking about nothing in particular until we finally made our way back to the restaurant parking area after getting shaved ice. He walked me to my car, lingering a little too close for comfort. "I'd like to see you again," he said. "I've liked getting to know you. I want to know more."

I wished I could say the same. There was nothing wrong with Chris. His fatal flaw was the fact he wasn't Ethan. "Give me a call," I said with a smile.

It was my way of brushing him off. I knew a third date was unlikely. I tried once and then convinced myself a second date would change things. It didn't. I was simply not interested.

I moved to grab my doorhandle, but he stopped me. When I looked up to see what else he wanted to say, he kissed me. Stunned and confused by his sudden bold move, I did nothing. I didn't kiss him back, but I didn't push him away. I just waited for it to be over. Chris pulled back with a smile on his face.

I opened my eyes and looked at him. There was still no spark. Nothing. It was like kissing a stranger. "Ava," Chris said with a laugh.

I frowned at him. Now that the shock was wearing off, I was irritated. He didn't get to just kiss me. I knew I had not given him any signals suggesting I wanted a kiss. I shook my head and was about to tell him this would never work when something behind him caught my eye. It was Ethan. He was looking our way, and judging by the look on his face, he didn't look happy.

I felt like I had just been caught cheating. I didn't need to feel that way. Ethan and I weren't together. We were the very opposite of together. We weren't anything. We slept together a couple of times and that was that. We meant nothing to each other. He was free to date who he wanted. I was free to kiss anyone I chose to, including the guy pushing into my personal space like he thought he might get another kiss. I didn't owe Ethan shit. I should kiss Chris. Ethan was not my boyfriend.

He wasn't even an ex. I didn't have to hide the fact I was out with another man.

Then why did the look on his face cause me physical pain? Why did I feel so guilty?

Chapter Four

Ethan

I parked the car and scanned the street. There was supposed to be a shipping store that was open all night. I had documents that had to get back to New York. I spotted the store and made my way down the sidewalk. The place was busy. There were people everywhere. I noticed a car that looked familiar. It didn't take long before I placed it. Ava was walking toward the car with a tall, blond man right behind her. I couldn't explain why, but I moved out of the way, taking refuge behind a palm tree in order to spy.

I couldn't hear what they were saying, but it was evident they had been on a date. Ava had her date look. She was wearing a pair of capris with wedge sandals. Even from where I stood, I could tell she had put on more makeup than she normally wore. If I tried hard enough, I could practically smell her. She always smelled a little of coconut with some vanilla.

The man was young. With the clean-cut high and tight haircut, I pegged him for Navy. My jealousy was inching up by the second. This was exactly the kind of man she was supposed to be with. He was Navy, which she would be drawn to because of her father. I was surprised she hadn't been swept off her feet earlier by some hotshot Navy dude. That's what she deserved. She should be with a man who would treat her right, give her a bunch of babies, and live happily ever after.

But damn if I wasn't jealous as hell. I wished I could have been the one she could rely on. The man who could make her happy. It just wasn't meant to be. History had put us on opposite sides of a fight she didn't even know she was in. If and when she found out who I was, she would want nothing to do with me. There was no chance we could ever have that happily ever after.

The man leaned in and kissed her. I flinched, exhaling sharply like I was in pain. I was. I couldn't believe how badly it hurt to see her with another man. I couldn't stick around. Pushing away the hurt and jealousy, I moved out from behind the tree and headed for the shipping store.

I quickly took care of mailing the package. All I wanted to do was get back to the rental house. I wanted to hide away with a bottle of something. I wanted to dull the pain and just forget all about the drama happening back in New York. When I opened the door to walk out, I tried to will myself invisible. I wanted to slink back to my car without her seeing me.

"Ethan!"

"Fuck," I muttered under my breath. She had seen me. I could walk faster and look like a fool. Or I could stop and pretend I had not seen her and the guy kissing. I blew out a breath, knowing there was no way I was going to get out of the situation unscathed.

I turned around to see her rushing toward me. I looked over her shoulder. The guy was gone. Was he waiting in the car? At her apartment? Was she fucking him? The thought made me see red.

"Yes?" I asked coolly.

"He's a friend," she blurted out.

"Excuse me?"

"The guy I was with," she said. "It's not what you think."

"I don't know what you're talking about," I lied.

"Don't lie," she shot back. "I saw you. You saw me."

"Whatever," I snapped. I had to get back.

"You're pissed."

"I'm not anything," I said. "Fuck who you want. It's not like we have anything going."

Her mouth dropped open. "You asshole."

"I don't know what you want, Ava." I shrugged. "Call me an asshole if that makes you feel better. You chased after me, not the other way around. I have no say about who you take to bed. I was just a passing fancy."

"Stop it," she scolded. "Don't act like I'm whoring around. You know that's bullshit. I could be kissing you, but you made it pretty clear you thought I was nothing but some floozy using you."

"I didn't think that," I shot back.

"You thought I stole from you," she hissed. "Why in the hell would I steal from you? You made me feel about two inches tall. You put on this big sob story about everyone using you and how miserable you were back there. I'm such a damn fool. I fell for your story."

"It wasn't a story," I said.

She rolled her eyes. "You assume everyone knows who you are or even cares. I didn't know you from Adam when you showed up here. To think I would ever sell information about you to anyone is asinine. I can't believe you thought so little about me to even think I would do something like that. All I can say is, shame on you. You ruined something that could have been really good. If you're miserable, it's because you want to be. No wonder you're hiding here. If this is how you treat people, you deserve whatever has happened."

She was being pretty damn harsh. "I don't treat people any which way. I apologized. Period."

"And that's good enough for you." She snorted. "People like you just assume everyone else should just accept your apology and pretend everything is fine. Little people like me are supposed to just be so grateful you deigned to apologize at all. What you did was abysmal. I could almost understand you making such a disgusting accusation if we hadn't spent time together."

"Sex," I said. "We had sex."

"Thank you for making it sound cheap," she hissed.

"I'm not making it cheap," I said, trying to soften it.

"I hate that I gave even five minutes of my time," she snapped with such vehemence I took a step back. "I gave you four minutes too many. I don't know how you operate in your normal world, but I was raised not to accuse without facts. And if you were going to accuse someone of something horrific, you should at least give them the chance to get a word in. You are clearly used to saying your piece and people just accept it. I'm not one of your employees or someone you can just push around. You can't just accuse me of something like that and think an apology is going to make it better. You are the reason I left New York."

"Me?" I asked with confusion. I didn't miss the fact there were some people watching us. We were making quite the scene.

"You. People like you. I had to live with your kind for too long. Rich, entitled people just think they can say and do whatever they want with no consequences. Honestly, I'm glad I learned who you were before things went any further. You are one of my biggest mistakes. Good luck with the rest of your life. I hope I never have to see you again. Richard will be handling any problems you might have with the house. You can leave a message and I'll send him over. I don't expect there to be any reason for you to call me. Ever. I cannot wait for you to be off my island. You deserve the people you're trying to hide from. Take one last look, asshole, because you will not be touching this again."

She spun on her heel and walked away back to her car. The man she'd been kissing appeared out of nowhere. He put his hand on her shoulder and looked to be consoling her. I watched with rage burning through me. She wasn't going to hear me out. I supposed I had burned that bridge. I hurt her. I got it. I wouldn't want to talk to me either. I turned, walked to my car, and sped away with my heart shattered.

As if the day wasn't already shot to shit, I got a call from Lucas. I could only imagine what news he had for me. "What?" I answered. "Please tell me the world is going to explode."

"Not yet, but that might be something we could pray for," he said dryly. "It would certainly make life easier."

"What happened now?" I asked with resignation.

"I talked to Collin," he said.

"And?"

"And he is claiming he's been framed," he said. "He claims this is all a big misunderstanding. Said it wasn't his drugs. You know the story."

"Yes, I know." I sighed.

I opened the bottle of scotch and poured a glass. I took a drink, feeling the burn and then topped it off again. I was caught in a snowball rolling downhill with no chance of it slowing down. It just kept getting worse. I was afraid to think about what might come next. A conviction. A lawsuit. It was hard to guess.

"There's been reporters camped outside the building," he said. "The more information and rumors, the worse it's getting."

"They're looking for me," I stated.

"Yep," he replied. "I've been asked over and over. Reporters have followed me to my car. There was some asshole waiting outside my building for me. It's best you stay away. This shit is getting ugly."

"I'm sorry you're dealing with this," I said. "This is on me."

"It's on Collin," he said.

"What's the vibe in the office?" I asked.

"Not good," he replied. "Not good at all. People are pissed."

"Fuck," I groaned. "Anyone quit?"

"Yes."

I took another drink. "How many?"

"We lost two in accounting and one in HR," he said. "I think we need to consult an outside firm."

"What do you mean?"

"We need help," he answered. "We're up a creek right now. We have to do damage control. We haven't even hit the height of this storm yet. If there is a connection found between Collin and those drugs, it's going to get bad. I've made a couple of calls to some PR firms. Basically, a cleanup crew. We are going to get buried. Our team isn't ready for this. This is not what they are trained for. It's going to cost some money, but it will be worth it in my opinion."

"Have you talked with the board about it?" I asked. "I'm hesitant to make a decision. I know they're not fond of me. I don't want to piss anyone off. I'm here, you're there. You're on the ground."

"I'm telling you we need to do this," he said. "I don't think this is a decision for the board. You're the CEO."

"For now," I muttered.

"Give me the green light," he said. "They'll need to talk to you and give you information about what to say. They'll want to find out what you know. Think of them as an attorney. There will be a contract and NDAs in place. We have to do this."

I hated bringing in someone to fix our problems. I hated that we had been reduced to this. "Fine," I said. "Do it. Have them email me. I'm not answering my phone to numbers I don't recognize."

"I'll pass it along," he said. "What happened with the girl?"

"Ava?"

"Yes," he said. "Please tell me you're not messing with her. We've got enough problems."

"Trust me, she doesn't want anything to do with me," I replied. "She won't be a problem."

"And you sound pretty pissed about that," he said.

"I'm not happy about it."

"I'm sorry, but there are a million other women you can fall in love with," he said. "She's not one of them. She's the one woman you cannot have. Trust me, you can't add to your troubles. Your plate is full."

"I know. I get it. She's out of my life."

We talked a few more minutes before hanging up. I felt like I had been through a ringer. I was so ready for this shit to be over. I was seriously considering my life choices.

Chapter Five

Ava

I wanted to ignore the phone call, but it was time to shut the guy down. I would let him down easy, but it had to be done. After a night of thinking and contemplation, I had made the decision to stop seeing Chris. He was a nice guy, but he made it pretty clear he was looking for something I wasn't able to give. His kiss last night made that abundantly clear. Chris would find another local to have a brief romance with. I knew there were plenty of young women who would love to move to the mainland. He could go out with one of them. I was not interested.

"Hello," I answered with a sad smile.

"There you are," he replied. "How are you?"

"I'm fine, Chris."

"Are you sure?" he asked. "You looked pretty upset last night. Who was that guy?"

"He's just someone I know," I said.

"An ex?" he pressed.

I didn't appreciate the questioning. "Chris, he's just a guy I've met a few times."

"Okay, I don't want to pry, I just wanted to make sure you were okay," he said. "Are you doing anything tomorrow night? I finish work early. I was thinking we could go to a place I heard about. They host some amazing luaus."

I was pretty sure Chris forgot I actually lived in Oahu. Going to a luau was an average Tuesday for me. Technically, I didn't even go to them because if you'd seen ten, you'd seen a thousand. I understood that it was exciting for him and I loved that he wanted to do all the things with me. It was just not clicking for me.

"Chris, you're a good man," I said. "I've enjoyed out time together, but I'm just not ready for this."

"For what?" he asked. "A date?"

"Dating in general," I told him.

He was quiet for several seconds. "I see."

"I think you're a good guy, Chris," I said. I hated the speech. I sounded like every other person dumping someone. It was cliché and I knew it sounded trite. It was all very true. "I know that sounds lame, but I promise, it's true. I am just not in a the right place for dating."

"Because of the guy," he said with a sigh.

"Yes," I finally admitted. "I'm sorry. I had fun and I thought there might be a chance, but I'm just not there. I don't want to string you along. That's not fair to you."

"I get it," he said. "It's a bummer. I liked you."

"I'm sorry," I said again.

"It's cool. Thanks for letting me know. Good luck with the other guy."

"Trust me, there is nothing with the other guy," I scoffed. "I need time to put all of that behind me."

"I understand," he replied. "You're a fun girl, Ava. I hope you find a man who treats you right. I'll see you around."

"Thanks."

I put the phone down after ending the call and fell back into a weird sense of sadness and loss. I never had Ethan to lose, but it felt like that. For the briefest moment, there had been hope. I thought maybe I could be with him. I let myself fantasize about a relationship that would never happen. I was mourning the loss of something I never had. Something that had only been a figment of my imagination. I was so sad he wasn't the man I thought he might be.

We had a week of fun and laughter. I was certain we had developed a friendship. The sex was good, but it wasn't everything. I had felt a connection to him. At least I thought it was a connection. He changed overnight. I went to bed with one man and woke up with another.

For him to have the audacity to get angry at me being with Chris was bullshit. I saw the look on his face. He had definitely been angry. He could say otherwise, but I had seen the way he was looking at me. His jaw was clenched, and his eyes were flashing with anger. The man had been furious. He made me feel like I had cheated on him when I had done nothing wrong. He was the one who flipped out on me. Did he actually think I was just going to crawl back to him because he muttered he was sorry? The guy had flipped out over something that never happened. Chris was a good guy. I doubted he would ever do anything like that.

But dammit, I was hung up on Ethan and I would never find out what kind of man Chris was because I couldn't get past Ethan. I should have known better. I did know better. I knew not to mess with men like Ethan. I had been there, done that way too many times not to have learned a lesson. It was a little embarrassing to still be trying to figure it out. When I left New York, I left my family, my life, and the guys I tried valiantly to date. The one guy I thought was different than the rest showed me his true colors—Jeff. He had pretended to be someone he wasn't. It was our senior year of college and I was in the phase of making plans for my future. We talked about sharing that future.

I would never forget the day he showed me his true colors.

I wiped a tear from my eye and leaned my head against Jeff's shoulder. "I don't know what we're supposed to do," I said with a hiccup. "My mom is freaking out. My sister's college fund is gone. I'm just glad my tuition has already been paid."

"You don't have a trust fund?" Jeff asked.

The question wasn't unfounded. He and my circle of friends were all wealthy. Most had trust funds or didn't have to have them because their parents kept them flushed with cash. "No." I sniffled. "I did, but he took it."

"Your grandfather?" he asked.

"Yes. It's a mess. I don't know what's happening. My mom said the family was broke. I don't know if that means broke as in, we have to sell the condo in Aspen or broke as in she might have to get an actual job."

"Damn," Jeff said. "That's harsh."

I leaned away and looked up at him. He wasn't exactly conveying warmth and comfort. I had not seen him since the whole scandal broke. Then my grandfather died. Jeff had conveniently been too busy studying to go to the funeral with me. He was cold. Like I was some stranger on the subway leaning against him.

"My mom is crushed," I said.

"Yeah." He nodded.

"Jeff, what's wrong?" I asked. "Why are you acting weird?"

He rubbed his hands against his thighs. "I didn't want to do this now when you're dealing with so much, but—"

I hopped up from the couch and stared at him. I knew what was coming. I could feel it. "Don't you dare," I hissed.

"Ava, my family wants me to marry a girl who can help me get to the governorship," he said. "Your family is embroiled in scandal. I can't be attached to that."

"My family isn't embroiled in scandal," I shot back. "We're broke. Newsflash, being poor isn't scandalous."

"You know what I mean," he said. "I have to maintain a certain image. Besides, you're going to feel weird being around all of us. We're rich, you're not."

My mouth gaped. "Are you kidding me right now?"

"I'm sorry." He shrugged and got to his feet. "I just think it's best we end this now. I mean, it's not like we're going to get married or anything. I need to think about my future."

"You are a piece of shit," I said with disgust. "You are actually dumping me because I'm not rich. That's classy."

"It wasn't really working out," he muttered. "I mean you're hot and stuff, but you're not really First Lady material."

"Wow," I breathed in disbelief. I wasn't even hurt anymore. I was pissed. I wanted him out of my life. For good.

"Uh, I should probably tell you now before you see us at school," he said and shoved his hands into his pockets.

"Tell me what?"

"Me and Carly are seeing each other," he murmured.

My head was swimming. "You're seeing Carly? Carly the diamond heiress?"

"Yeah," he said with a nod. "When you left, she was there for me."

"I left two fucking weeks to deal with my mother! There for you! Are you kidding? What exactly was she there for you for? What tragedy were you going through?"

"You," he said like it actually made sense in his head. "You and I were falling apart. She comforted me."

"She fucked you," I spat. "You and I weren't falling apart. My family was, which meant you didn't want to have anything to do with me if I wasn't one of society's darlings. I knew you were shallow, but damn, Jeff, this is next level. You are seriously the biggest piece of shit I've ever met. You're a waste of space. Get out. I never want to see you again."

"You don't have to be a bitch about it," he said. "You know we have nothing in common now."

"Yeah, I get it." I walked to the door of my very nice apartment that had been paid for by my mother's family. "Leave."

"Please don't be all weird at school," he begged. "I don't want you to make a scene. Carly doesn't want you telling people I was cheating on you with her."

"I don't give a shit what Carly wants," I snapped. "You two deserve each other."

"Okay, that's cool, whatever. I want you to know I did care about you."
"Yes, I'm sure you did," I said dryly. "You cared about getting laid."
He paused at the doorway. "You don't have to be bitter."
"And you don't have to be a lousy lay," I said and slammed the door in his face.

The memory was just as fresh and raw as it had been the day he'd done what he did. It wasn't just Jeff who had dumped me. All of my so-called friends had distanced themselves. Only Andrea had stuck by my side. She had been kind and loyal. I wasn't even sad Jeff and I broke up. I didn't love him, but I had been young and naïve and believed I was special to him. I was another notch on his bedpost. Last I heard, he was dating some shipping magnate's daughter. He was looking to marry rich. He didn't care about love. He was one of the main reasons I shunned that whole lifestyle. I never wanted to be like him or any of those people.

Living in Hawaii had been a breath of fresh air. It had renewed my belief in humanity. Not everyone was like the people I had lived with for too long. The people I had surrounded myself with here in Hawaii were amazing. They didn't have a lot, but that wasn't what they cared about. They lived in paradise and appreciated the little things. They didn't care if you had a million dollars in the bank or ten dollars. I loved the family atmosphere.

It was too bad Ethan didn't give himself the chance to see what true happiness looked like. You couldn't buy it. He was doomed to live a life of distrust and frustration because he chose to assume the worst in everyone. It was sad he was going to be left cold and lonely, but I couldn't save him. He wasn't my problem. I didn't want to see him again. He was nothing but heartache. I saw it the moment I laid eyes on him, but I let my guard down. I was a sucker. He needed help and my hero complex sprang into action. I rushed to save him and made him my project.

Now, I just wanted him out of my life. I didn't want to think about him again. I certainly didn't want to see him again.

Except I did. That's what pissed me off the most. I'd been waging this internal war. I wanted a magic pill to forget all about him.

Chapter Six

Ethan

It was a mistake. I shouldn't have done it. Lucas told me not to do it. But I did it. I was bored and it was pouring rain. I was stuck inside with nothing to do except think and dwell on stupid shit. At some point, I ended up on the internet. I didn't have social media, but it wasn't like I had to be a registered user to see the shit being said about me and my family.

The rumors circulating were pretty impressive. Some of these people should consider writing fiction. I clicked on an article on a gossip site. A picture of me taken a couple of years ago was front and center. I looked like I was in pain with my face twisted. Technically, I was in pain at the moment the picture was taken. I had just left the gym and pulled a hamstring. The picture was not flattering. I wasn't surprised they used the worst picture possible. It matched the headline.

"Ethan Mitchell's whereabouts raise concern," I read aloud. I took a drink and continued to read the article that was seriously a work of fiction. There should be a law that prohibited the kind of bullshit I was reading.

"Sources close to the family say Ethan overdosed the same night and has been recovering in an undisclosed location." I started laughing. "The source also reveals the CEO's health is grave and there is a chance he won't be able to maintain his position."

I rolled my eyes and clicked off the article. The rumor mill was pretty impressive. There were stories about Collin selling drugs. According to more sources, Collin was part of a cartel and I was being held hostage until Colin paid them. There seemed to be a real infatuation with my whereabouts. It was funny but not funny. It was disturbing they were so invested in where I was. I was not involved. I didn't need to be there.

Sitting inside on a dreary day would have been so much better with company. I would have loved to have spent it with Ava. We could have made dinner and hung out in front of the TV. A little kissing would have been nice. But that wasn't going to be. She made it clear she wanted nothing to do with me. I couldn't try to convince her otherwise if I wanted to keep her out of my family's dirty business.

I shut down the computer and refilled my drink. While staring out the window and contemplating life in general, my phone started ringing. The phone calls weren't stopping. I was thousands of miles away and it was like I was sitting at home in New York.

I glanced down at the screen. It was my mother. Again. I talked to her earlier. Unless Collin had been arrested, I didn't see what there was to talk about. I let it go to voicemail. "Three, two, one," I murmured. Just like she always did, she called right back. I wasn't surprised. That's how this went. She would call me over and over until I picked up. I could turn off my phone, which was what I usually did, or deal with it. She would continue to blow up my phone and email until I picked up.

"Yes, Mother?" I answered with a sigh.

"Ethan," she mumbled my name.

She was drunk. Or stoned. It was hard to say. She'd been hitting the pills pretty hard since the whole thing started. "Are you on your way?" she asked.

"On my way where?" I asked.

"Home," she slurred the word.

"Mom, no, I'm not coming home."

"How could you abandon us?" she whined. "Why would you leave us at a time when I needed you the most? My family is falling apart. I'm questioning everything. Was I a bad mother?"

I rolled my eyes. This was the typical conversation. She would moan and groan and want me to tell her she was a great mom. That would be a lie. She was an acceptable mother. She never really leaned into the mom thing.

"I don't know what you want me to say." I sighed.

"I want you to say you'll come home! Do you know what they are saying about us? About you?"

"I don't care," I said. "It's not the truth. People have gossiped about us forever. That's nothing new. We can't control what people think or say about us."

"I've been ostracized," she wailed. "I'm not even welcome to attend meetings for the charities I sit on the boards. I was asked to stay away out of fear I would stain the reputations of the charities. Do you know what this is going to do to my reputation? All my years of hard work are just gone!"

"You just need to ride it out," I told her. "It will blow over soon."

"The damage is done," she groaned. "I don't know what I'm going to do. I won't be able to show my face in public. I'll never get an invitation to a party or anything again. It's over."

The woman was an expert at manipulating a situation to make her a victim. She wanted everyone to fawn over her and give her the attention she felt she needed. She seemed to forget it wasn't just her who was suffering. We were all dealing with the fallout. If the company continued to lose money, people were going to lose their jobs. People who couldn't afford to not have a job. I wasn't exactly coming through the thing unscathed. My face was the one being splashed all over the news. I was the one who was being gossiped about.

"I don't know what you want me to say," I said with a sigh. "We're all dealing with this. Collin made some pretty bad choices in his life. He's been making bad choices for years and no one has done shit to stop him."

"Don't talk like that," she scolded. "Your father and I have done everything in our power to help him. We've sent him to the best rehabs in the world."

"But did you ever cut him off?" I asked. "He has access to money. Why would he stop doing the thing he loves when he doesn't have to? You and Dad practically forced me to leave the military to go to work at the company. I've poured my heart and soul into the company. I've sacrificed my whole life to keep that place growing and thriving. Every quarter I've increased profits which increases your bank account. Do you know what I've given up to keep the family business running?"

"You've lived a very good life," she chided.

"I'm living a very lonely life," I shot back.

"We've tried to set you up with a number of young women who would make a good wife for you," she said.

I shook my head. She wasn't going to get it. Her small mind wouldn't allow it. "Yeah, because that's what I want, a blue-blooded pony to produce the perfect children and then spend her days at the spa. Love doesn't matter, right?"

"Stop," she said. "This is serious."

My mother didn't get love. She might have liked us, but she didn't love us like a mother loved her children. We were props. Accessories. When we started to get older, we weren't quite as cute. Our value to her became based on our prospects on the marriage market. She wanted to be able to plan an extravagant wedding that would attract lots of press. She'd be queen for a day.

"Look, I can't stop this," I said. "I can't fix it. We are at the mercy of the press and the police. Then we'll be at the mercy of the lawyers that are surely to get involved very soon."

"You need to be here," she said. "It's just making this all so much worse. Have you seen the things they are saying about you?"

"Yep."

"We need you here," she groaned. "I need you."

"Mom, it's better if I'm not there," I explained for the third time. "The lawyers wanted me as far from the situation as possible. We all knew it was going to hit the fan. If I was there, it would just be worse. The goal was to put some distance between the scandal and the company. If I'm there, I become a part of the story."

"You're already a part of the story!" she shot back. "You're just hiding because you don't want your name associated with any of this."

"You're right." I laughed humorlessly. "I don't, but no one is letting me forget who my family is. The company is hemorrhaging money right now. Stocks are selling off. If I'm there, it shines more light on the company. I'm laying low."

"You're hiding," she mumbled. "Your father thinks you are as well. It's really unlike you to abandon anyone, let alone your own family."

"I haven't abandoned anyone," I replied. "I'm doing all I can to keep things running smoothly. Lucas is dealing with a PR firm. I've been on the phone with them for hours trying to do damage control. Your anger is being pointed in the wrong direction. I'm not the one you should be mad at. Where's Collin?"

"Stop, you know we can't have Colling running around," she said.

"Exactly," I said. "You've got him tucked away. He's probably holed up with a few women and a lot of drugs. Have you checked on him?"

"Stop it! How dare you say such things about him. That's your little brother."

She was clearly drunk. "Yeah, that's what you tell me," I muttered.

"What happens if he goes to jail?" she sobbed. "Our family will never recover."

"Yep, that will be bad," I said dryly.

"This isn't a joke, Ethan!"

"No, it isn't, Mom," I shot back. "I can't go to work and take care of the company I've poured my time and energy into because my little brother got high and may have inadvertently killed his friend. I can't go into the office and be the CEO. I can't look after the employees who work for us and are probably feeling pretty nervous right about now. You aren't the only one with a stain. We're all screwed because Collin got high! Again!"

I heard her sobbing and immediately felt bad. "I'm sorry," I said. "We're all frustrated. I'm doing what I can to protect the company. If I'm in New York, my face gets splashed around. I'm the face of the company. We don't need people associating the company with Collin. We can't stop it, but we can limit it."

"Do you really think that will work?" she asked.

Her voice was low. It sounded like she was on the verge of passing out. "I don't know," I told her. "The lawyers and the new PR firm think it's the best for now. The PR people are working out a strategy to bring me back. Until then, I'm staying away."

"Where are you?"

"I'm in Hawaii," I finally told her.

"At least you're in the country," she mumbled.

I didn't say anything for a few minutes. I was pretty sure I could wait her out. I waited until I didn't hear her anymore. I ended the call after I was sure she had passed out. I wondered where my father was. He was sleeping on the job. Mom was fucked up. Collin was probably fucked up. Dad was probably locked in the den with a bottle of scotch. I knew why they wanted me there. I was going to be the cleanup crew. They wanted me to smile and nod and say all the right things to get the press off their backs. They wanted me to flash a smile and charm them. It had worked in the past, but I didn't think a smile was going to make it go away.

This was bigger than a smile. This was apocalyptic. The worst part was we were just at the beginning of it. Even the PR firm was bracing me for the real shitstorm that was to come. If Collin was actually arrested, I could pretty much count out ever going back to work. I would have to take the money I had in the bank and walk away.

I was still trying to figure out why that was a bad thing. Why was I trying to prevent that from happening?

Chapter Seven

Ava

"Ruger, woah," I ordered the massive German Shepherd. He was tugging on the leash hard enough to make me trip while walking.

He barked and skipped a few steps. I tried to plan my walks with dogs that could keep up with one another. It wasn't always possible. "Gigi, I'm sorry," I said to the small dachshund that was in a full sprint trying to keep up with Ruger's pace.

"Good morning, Ava," one of the shop owners greeted.

"Good morning."

"I think Ruger has grown another two feet." He laughed.

"Would you believe he's not even a year old," I said.

I didn't get the chance to stop and talk. The dogs demanded we keep walking. I made it to the dog park and let them run for a while. Ruger was the star of the show as always. He was a handsome dog and people loved him. He was huge and scary, but he was the dopiest dog I had ever met. Little Gigi scared me more than Ruger.

One of the other dog walkers moved to sit by me on the bench. "How are you?" she asked.

"Good, you?"

She smiled. "Tired," she answered. "I just started a new job at the clinic."

"Did you get your nursing license?"

She nodded. "Yes, finally."

"Congratulations. Good for you."

"Thanks," she said. "Do you mind if I pass your name onto the hotel?"

I tried not to cringe. Extra work wasn't a terrible thing, but I was stretched pretty thin. "Sure, but I don't know how much I can take on."

"I'll let them know," she assured me.

"How much longer are you going to work for the hotel?" I asked.

"This is my last week," she replied. "I'm actually going to miss some of the regulars but I'm not going to miss picking up dog shit."

"No kidding." I laughed. "Or getting to a store or going on a date and pulling out poop bags from my purse."

"Are you going to keep doing it?" she asked. "You said once you got the other rental up and running, you were going to cut back."

"I don't know." I sighed. "I thought I was but now I'm thinking I might keep doing it to pay down some bills."

"Are you still seeing that guy?" she asked.

"What?" I asked and immediately felt guilty. "Who?"

"The tall, handsome guy," she replied. "I saw you guys at the beach. You looked busy so I left you alone."

She was talking about Ethan. "No," I said with a smile. "Not anymore."

"Ah, that's too bad. You looked really happy."

"He wasn't really a boyfriend or anything like that," I said. "Just a friend." I got up from the bench. "I better get these guys home. I've already been out longer than I expected. Good luck with your new job. I'm proud of you."

"Thank you."

I whistled and got the dogs leashed up again. On the way back, I thought about people seeing me out with Ethan. Everyone assumed he was my boyfriend. I hated that I looked like I got dumped by the slick New Yorker. It was a pride thing. There was a thing amongst us locals. At least I considered myself a local. Unless you were one of those people purposely looking for a little action with no strings, you stayed away from the visitors. Everyone knew they came in with their slick moves and liked to hook up with the locals. Then they went home and never thought twice about us.

I had never fallen for any of the bullshit before Ethan. He of all people was the one guy I let myself get involved with. He stood for everything I hated. I didn't understand why I let myself want him. He was such a prick. He thought of me as the vacation fling. I wondered if he was already on to another local. The thought made me want to scream at the top of my lungs. I wanted to rage against him. The other night I had gotten a lot off my chest, but since then, I had thought of so much more I wanted to say to him.

I told him I never wanted to see him again. That meant I couldn't very well tell him what I wanted to say.

Unless I could.

I dropped off the last dog and went home. "Roxy, talk me out of it," I said. "Tell me not to do it."

The dog cocked her head to the side and looked at me like I was crazy. I was crazy. I was being ridiculous. No good could come from telling him off. Again. But now that I had time to think about it, I wanted to know what he meant about leaking information. What information? I could Google him, but my internet was garbage and I knew I could not trust what I read online. I had been a part of that media circus once before. The lies that were told as the gospel truth were hurtful and ridiculous. I didn't want to read something about him and have it cloud my mind. Nothing was real. But I was curious. Was he a criminal? Was he trying to skip out on an accusation or criminal charges? I felt like it was something I should know. Was I harboring a criminal?

My mind was made up. "You should have tried harder to talk me out of it," I said to Roxy. "Now look what I'm going to do. I'm going to go make a damn fool of myself and start a bunch of drama. Last chance. Tell me not to do it."

She said nothing. Instead, she jumped on the couch and curled up in a ball in her spot. She was of no use. I needed a voice of reason. She was not it. I rubbed her head before grabbing my keys. I took off toward the rental with questions popping into my head in rapid succession. What did he do? Why was he on the outs with his family?

I got to the rental and didn't see the car in the driveway. If I was really naughty, I could let myself in and do a little snooping. It would be a huge violation of his privacy and our rental agreement. I had no business even being at the house. I knew the housekeeping portion was already handled. I got out of the car and stared at the front door. Before I could change my mind, the door opened with Ethan standing in the doorway.

"Shit," I muttered under my breath. No turning back.

"Ava?" he asked with confusion.

Seeing him handsome and shirtless pissed me off. I stomped forward and stopped a few feet in front of him. "What'd you do?" I asked.

"Excuse me?"

"You accused me of revealing your hiding spot," I said. "You were freaking out that I might be selling out your secrets. I already know you're hiding here. Tell me why."

"That's really none of your business," he said defiantly.

"I think it is," I argued. "You have accused me of stealing and ratting you out. You're in my house. I've spent countless hours with you. Am I in danger?"

"In danger of what?" he asked with a smirk.

"You. Are you a sexual predator?"

That was the wrong question. I couldn't even explain why the words came out of my mouth. He found it amusing. "I'm not sure what you consider to be a predator, but as far as I know, I've never been referred to as a predator. Except in business."

"What crime have you committed?" I asked.

"Why do you think I've committed a crime?" he asked with a laugh.

"Because you were pretty damn worried I sold out your whereabouts," I shot back. "You went batshit crazy and suggested I broke a few laws just to earn a few bucks. You have obviously done something. You said you're hiding from your family. I don't believe that. You're hiding from a lot more than just your family."

"You checked?" he asked with disappointment.

"No, but I can very easily, or you can just tell me."

He shrugged and folded his arms across his chest. "I don't see why you care," he said. "It's not like you're holding a torch for me. You seem to have moved on pretty quickly."

"Excuse me?"

"You got up on this high horse pretending you're this high and mighty local who would never stoop to messing with a tourist," he sneered. "What'd you tell me? I think it was something like you don't date, right? Was that it? You just do the Navy guys. It's not like I care, but you don't have to pretend. It's your thing."

"What in the actual hell are you talking about?" I snapped.

"The guy you were making out with," he said. "Were you seeing him and fucking me, or did you hop out of my bed and into his?"

I couldn't believe my ears. He walked into the house with that shitty smirk on his face. I wasn't about to let him walk away after he said all that. I went into the kitchen right behind him just in time to see him fill a glass with dark liquid. That explained his loose lips and insulting behavior.

"Are you drunk?" I asked with the proper accusation in my voice.

"Yep," he nodded. "I think I might be."

I rolled my eyes. "Figures."

"Let me guess, you have some kind of rule about that?" he asked. "Is it another one of the perfect Ava's rules? We all know you would never do anything so bad. You're perfect."

"You're an idiot," I said with a shake of my head. Yelling at him was no longer fun. He was drunk and stupid.

"I probably am." He nodded and took another long drink. "Where's your boyfriend? I'm guessing he's not going to appreciate you being here with me. Does he know about us? Or wait, I bet I'm your dirty little secret. You don't want any of your local friends knowing you got down and dirty with the guy from New York. You're too good for that."

"You're really drunk. And stupid."

"I would offer you a drink, but I think I remember you saying you didn't want to see me again," he said.

"He's not my boyfriend," I murmured.

His brows shot up. "Excuse me?"

"The guy, he's not my boyfriend. No, I haven't slept with him. Not that it's any of your business. It was just a date."

"Sure, of course," he replied with that stupid grin.

"I can't believe you think you get to talk shit about any of this," I said. "You're the asshole who went crazy. You assumed I had sold you out. You have something to hide. I thought I wanted to know, but now, I don't think so. I don't think I care. I'll just be glad when you're out of my life for good."

I started toward the door. "Run away, Ava! Run away. You can't accept I made a mistake. I apologized. You want to be mad and hate me, fine. I don't care. I've got much bigger problems than you."

I paused and turned to face him. There was a look on his face. He looked lost. And hurt. Every fiber of my being told me to go back to him and throw my arms around him. I didn't know what he was hiding from, but I knew he wasn't a criminal. He didn't hurt anyone. I felt that deep in my gut. But he wasn't telling me the truth and I could not put myself in a situation that left me hurting.

I walked out before I did something stupid.

Chapter Eight

Ethan

I felt like shit. It had been a long time since I had a hangover. Yesterday, I started drinking way early and continued drinking until I passed out. There was something about getting shitfaced. There was the hope you could fall asleep after drinking a bottle and all your troubles would just magically disappear. Unfortunately, the troubles were still there, and you were just left feeling like shit while dealing with the same troubles.

The drinking had been a last resort. I woke up to a slew of emails from Collin's lawyer and our family attorney. Things were getting worse. Indictments were being talked about. The DA's office was not talking, which was not good. It likely meant they were about to charge Collin with a crime. His lawyer was convinced they couldn't charge him with murder, but something was coming. My mother had gone off the deep end. My father was pissed at everyone except Collin.

It was all becoming too much. I could feel myself reaching a breaking point. It actually scared me a little. I didn't know what that looked like. What happened when I snapped? I honestly didn't know what that would mean. I had never really lost control. Ever. I had to be the level-headed one. My dad had a quick temper. My mom loved to drown her troubles in a cocktail of prescription meds. I was always the one steering our family through one crisis after another. If I broke, then what? The family and the company crumpled.

I had to get my head straight. Despite feeling like total shit, I put on my running shoes and jogged to the beach. I ran hard, pushing myself to the point of nearly puking. I kept running, even though my legs hurt and were shaking with every step. I kept trying to push away all thoughts of everything. I needed a clear head. I had to come up with a plan. There had to be a way to make all of this work.

I didn't jog back to the house. I barely dragged my ass up the stairs to take a shower. It wasn't exactly restorative, but I felt moderately better. I went downstairs to make myself coffee. I was hungry, but not hungry. I needed to eat and forced myself to choke down some toast and eggs. Fed and caffeinated, I should have felt better. Unfortunately, I didn't. Physically, yes but I was still feeling the weight of my burden.

I didn't want to do it but hiding from the drama wasn't doing me any good. I had to face the thing head-on. I made another cup of coffee and sat down at the table to do some work. As usual, I started with email. There were quite a few from different members of the board. I wasn't sure what they expected me to do. I tried to be polite, even though I knew they were looking to throw me out.

I called Lucas to check in with him. He was the only one giving it to me straight. "How bad is it?" I asked.

I heard him suck in a breath through his teeth. "It's not good."

"But how bad?"

"It just gets worse by the day," he replied. "By the hour, really. I never wanted to be a firefighter, but I think I understand what they do every day. I spend my days putting out fires. Big fires and little fires. All fucking day."

"I'm really sorry," I said. "I'm trying to do what I can on my end."

"The PR firm is putting together a media campaign," he said.

"Why?" I asked with a laugh. It almost felt like a joke. "Is it a pro-Collin piece? Try and make him look good?"

"No," he replied with a sigh. "I don't think there's enough money in the world to make him look good."

"Then what kind of campaign?" I asked. "I'm not interested in being the face of anything."

"Not you," he said. "They want to distance your family from the company. The media will be focused on the company itself. Nothing about the Mitchell family. It's going to be about that park we just sponsored. I've been working with the team here. We want to up the donations. They're looking at a children's center and a hospital wing. It's more than the typical sponsorship, but we need to put the focus on the good works the company does."

"I like it," I said. "Do it."

"The board is putting up a fight. They think we're trying to buy goodwill."

"We are," I commented with a sardonic laugh.

"They're worried it's going to look obvious."

"So?" I replied. "It sounds like the board is hoping we'll fail. They seem pretty damn intent on making this situation worse."

"They smell blood in the water," he said.

"They're still working on getting me out." I said it as a statement. It wasn't really a question. I knew it was coming.

"Did you see the drop in the stock today?" he asked as if to prove the point.

"Yes. I know. I know shit is bad. I'm doing all I can."

"I know," he said. "I'm sorry you're stuck dealing with this bullshit. I can only imagine how your family is taking this. They're waiting for their favorite son to swoop in and save the day."

"Something like that," I muttered.

"You need to put your foot down," he continued. "They've been relying on you to save their asses over and over. Collin is deadweight. I know he's your brother, but damn, dude. He's taking everyone down. If he does get charged with this, it opens the door to so much more. Wannabe sleuths are already digging. They're going to find out about the rehab stints, and the drunk driving, and everything else. It's going to blowback hard on your parents, but you're going to catch some of the shit as well. They're going to look for anything that makes your family look bad. I guarantee you there are going to people climbing out of the woodwork to claim Collin did this or that."

It was what I had already been told. The PR firm had been trying to prepare me for just about anything. They wanted to know the dirty details of Collin's past. I refused to spill the goods. If they asked something, I confirmed or denied it. I trusted no one, not even the people who were supposedly working to help the situation.

"Let me know what the campaign looks like," I said. "I don't know that there is much more than they can do but we'll go with it."

"I have to ask—" he started.

"No," I answered, already knowing exactly what it was he was looking for.

"I'm just trying to look out for you," he came back.

"Trust me, Ava wants nothing to do with me. The few times we've talked, it has not been pleasant. She hates me."

"Good," he said. "Not good, but good."

"I get it," I replied. "I'm staying away from her. For my own health and safety. Trust me when I say I'm not her favorite person. She's made that very clear."

"I know it's not what you want, but it's for the best."

"Yeah, yeah," I muttered. "I'll talk to you later."

I ended the call and tried to focus on more work tasks. I did a few DocuSigns, but my head wasn't in it. I closed down the laptop and stared out the window into the backyard. The rain had cleared out and it was a beautiful day. I didn't want to spend another day cooped up in the house. I had to get out and do something. My body could not tolerate another day of drinking. My psyche couldn't take being stuck inside four walls.

I opened the laptop once again and did a quick Google search for places to hike. It made me smile not to see any of the places Ava had taken me to see. Clicking through the pictures from other travelers proved her secret spots were better than any of the touristy spots. I found a waterfall that looked somewhat interesting and lowkey. I put the address into my map app and hoped like hell I had service long enough to get me all the way to the waterfall. And I hoped the roads were decent enough for the Porsche to navigate.

I put on the shoes I bought last week specifically for hiking. I opened the front door and was assaulted with a cacophony of shouting. Stunned and confused, I blinked several times. That's when it dawned on me—I wasn't seeing straight because there were flashes going off in my face.

"Ethan, is Collin with you?"

"Are you going to get your brother out of the country?"

"Were you at the party? Did you do the same drugs?"

"Are you recovering from an overdose?"

I stepped back inside and slammed the door shut. I locked it just in case someone got it in their head they could walk in. A flash went off in the room. "Fuck," I growled and quickly lowered the shades.

I couldn't stay in the house. I needed to get away. I rushed to the back of the house and peeked out the window. I didn't see anyone. I opened the door and waited just inside. When I didn't hear any shouting or see camera flashes, I took a tentative step outside. I had explored the area a bit. Going to the beach wasn't an option. I couldn't get to the car, which meant I was on foot.

I felt exposed but I had to get out. There was no way I could stay inside the house with the mob outside. It made me feel like a zoo animal. I quietly closed the door behind me and darted towards the tall bushes that framed the backyard. I stuck to the inside of the bushes. Once I reached a point where I would be exposed, I ran like hell. I hopped over the low fence that ran along the back of the property and raced down the single lane road. I stopped at the edge of the road and debated which way to go. One direction would lead me to the main road. The other led me into a neighborhood. Straight would put me in thick foliage, but I knew there was a road on the other side. I was going to have to call a ride.

I would take refuge at a hotel until I could find somewhere to go. I needed to get back to the house to get my stuff, but not now. I pulled my phone from my pocket and ended up staring at the screen. Who the hell was I going to call? I could call an Uber, but what if that person knew who I was? They would alert the press to where I was dropped off. I reached for my wallet, only to find it wasn't there.

"Fuck me," I groaned.

I must have left it in the bedroom. I had my keys to the car and my phone. I couldn't rent a hotel room if I wanted to. I stared up at the sky in search of divine intervention. The one person I knew in this place hated me. She made it very clear she wanted nothing to do with me. But I was desperate. What choice did I have? I could go back and face the vultures. I could get in the car and drive to the airport with a pack of hyenas on my tail. That did not sound appealing.

I looked back toward the house and debated what to do. If only Lucas could somehow send me a chopper to lift me up and carry me away.

Chapter Nine

Ava

"Assholes," I muttered and picked up another condom wrapper. "Animals."

I did all the cleaning for my rentals. Sometimes, people were great, and it was hard to tell anyone had even been in the place. Then there were people who completely trashed the rentals. I had spent the last two hours picking up beer cans and garbage in general. I scrubbed the kitchen from top to bottom and did my best to remove the stains from the rug in the living room. There was sand everywhere. The place was a fucking mess.

I vacuumed and sprayed the mattress with Lysol. I probably should have burned it. I didn't want to imagine what happened in the room. I finished remaking the bed and sprayed a little more Lysol for good measure. The bathroom was my last place to clean. I was so not looking forward to it.

I stared at the bathroom. The shower curtain had been torn down. The toilet seat had dried pee all over it. Someone had apparently puked and missed the toilet bowl. I supposed I should have been glad they attempted to clean it up. It wasn't going to clean itself. I opened the package of yellow gloves. This was one of the jobs that required I throw the gloves away after use.

I got busy scrubbing the tub and putting up a new shower curtain. Halfway through scrubbing the toilet, my phone rang. I ignored it, determined to finish the cleaning job. I was definitely not going to touch my phone with the gloves. And once I took the gloves off, they were going directly to the trash. I wiped down the sink and my phone started ringing again.

"Dammit," I muttered. I pulled off the gloves and dropped them in the trash. The phone was still ringing while I quickly washed my hands. When I pulled it from my pocket, I saw the name on my screen and considered tossing the thing in the trash as well.

The phone stopped ringing. I couldn't imagine what Ethan wanted now. The only reason he would call was if there was something wrong with the house. I was pretty sure he wouldn't call for anything else. It was clear we weren't friends. I had responsibilities that I couldn't shirk because I didn't like someone. I had to be a grownup.

When he called right back, I knew it was serious. "What?" I answered rudely.

"I need help," he said.

"I don't know why you're calling me," I replied with disgust.

"Look, I know you hate me," he started. "But I'm in trouble. You're the only person I could call."

"Are you stuck in the mud again?" I scoffed. "If you can call me, you can call a tow truck."

"I don't need a tow truck," he said, sounding desperate. "I need a ride. Please."

"Call a cab," I shot back.

"I can't," he hissed.

"I don't know why you thought I would be the person you called," I said. "I'm the very last person you should call."

"Maybe, but I'm hoping you can be the bigger person and help me out," he came back. "I wouldn't call if I had another option. You're the only one I can trust."

I snorted again. "Yeah, I saw how much you trust me."

"Ava, please," he said. "I just need a ride."

There was something in his voice that tugged at my heartstrings. I couldn't really leave him high and dry. That wasn't how I was. Yes, he was an asshole, but he was also a man. He was a guy in an unfamiliar place with no friends and no one to lean on. Could I really just leave him hanging?

"Why?" I asked with resignation.

He sighed again. "Please. I'll explain when you get here. Explain as much as I can."

"Oh, gee, more secrets," I said dryly.

"Can you come and get me or not?" he asked.

I wanted to say no. But dammit, I just couldn't walk away from someone in need. "Where are you?" I asked. "Do I need to call a tow truck?"

"No, I'm on foot," he muttered.

I was very confused. "Did you get in an accident?"

"No."

I heard a horn honking in the background. "Shit," he said. "Can you come and get me or not?"

It sounded like he was running. "I need to know where you are?"

"I'm on the move," he said out of breath. "Shit. Just meet me at the place I got my car stuck!"

The line went dead. That was weird. And alarming. I was actually worried about him. I left my cleaning supplies in the bathroom and grabbed my keys. I locked up and rushed out to my car. I realized I knew little about him, but it was actually alarming to hear him out of breath and running from someone. I had a hundred questions, but I doubted he was going to tell me much.

I made my way up the road noticing there was a little more traffic on the main road than usual. I avoided the ruts and holes in the road. I didn't see Ethan anywhere. I was going to be pissed if he sent me on a wild goose chase. I went up a little farther and was about to get really pissed when Ethan emerged from the bushes and trees along the side of the road.

He rushed to the passenger side and hopped in. I didn't know what I was witnessing. It felt wrong. "Go," he said.

"No. Not until you tell me what is going on."

"I'll explain later," he said. "We need to get out of here before they see us."

"Who is going to see us?" I asked. There was a twig stuck in his hair. Not thinking, I reached out and pulled it from his hair. "Are you actually running from someone?"

"A lot of someones," he answered. "Go. Please."

"Did you break the law? Commit a crime? Are the police after you?"

"I did not break any laws," he said. "The police are not after me."

I believed him. I didn't see him as a criminal. I made my way down the road. Ethan laid his seat as far back as it would go. I stopped and waited for a motorcycle to go by. They were going very, very slow. There was a camera hanging from around the driver's neck, which seemed just a little odd. It was pretty clear they were looking for someone. I had a feeling I had the someone in my car.

"Stay down," I said.

I was picking up on what was going on. The person on the motorcycle was a paparazzo. We got them from time to time when a celebrity showed up on the island. I drove in silence with my eyes on the rearview mirror. It was crazy that I slipped right into spy mode. Years of watching spy movies kicked in.

"Where am I taking you?" I asked him.

"I don't know," he answered.

"What does that mean?"

"It means my wallet is at the house," he said.

"Where is your car?" I asked.

"At the house," he answered.

"You do know this isn't normal," I said.

"Trust me, I know." He sighed.

"Where do you want me to take you?" I asked again.

"I know it's a lot to ask, and I have no right to impose on you, but can I crash at your place until I can find a way out of this mess?"

It was ridiculous. I should have said no. That was what a normal person would say. But not me. "You know this isn't right," I said.

"What part?"

"All of it," I said with a sigh.

"I know. I'm sorry that I had to call. I'm sorry that I need to lean on you to help me through this mess."

"Are you going to tell me what that mess is?" I asked.

I turned in the opposite direction of my apartment. My spy moves were in full gear. Ethan stayed down the entire time. I glanced over a few times. He was staring at nothing. Whatever was happening, it was bad. He looked lost. My heart went out to him. I was a sucker for someone down on their luck. I didn't care that he had accused me of stealing.

We got to my apartment, but he made no move to get out of the car. "Do you plan to stay in the car?"

"Did anyone follow you?" he asked.

"Do you mean the photographers?" I asked.

"Yes."

"No," I answered. "I made sure of it. Trust me, I don't know what mess you're caught up in, but I don't want it at my house."

"I know." He sighed. He sat the chair up and opened the door. I couldn't help but look over my shoulder to make sure we weren't followed. I unlocked my door and gestured for him to go inside.

I locked the door behind us and closed the blinds. He was standing in the living room like he didn't know if he should sit down or not. "Spill," I ordered.

"Ava, I can't say much," he said. "I know that's fucked up and you deserve the truth, but I can't tell you anything right now."

"That's not going to fly," I said. "You're asking me to give you safe harbor. I think it's pretty safe to say neither of us trusts the other. I deserve some kind of an explanation. You just put me in the middle of something."

"You're not in the middle of it," he said.

"Tell me or call someone to come and get you," I said firmly.

"My family is involved in some drama back in New York," he confessed. "It has nothing to do with me. Absolutely nothing."

"Then why in the world are there photographers here hunting you down to the point you are actually forced to run away?" I asked. "That doesn't pass the smell test."

"It's true," he said. "I've done nothing. This is guilt by association. They're looking for a story. They want to attach me to the bullshit back there."

"That's why you're here," I said with new understanding. "You were trying to hide from the press."

"Yes." He shrugged. "It's true. This isn't the first time something like this has happened. I knew what was coming. I swear to you I have nothing to do with what happened. I'm sick of being dragged into the messes they make. I do nothing but bust my ass for the family. Every time something happens, I'm left to clean up the mess. My name gets dragged through the mud. I didn't want to deal with it this time. I came here with the intention of hiding out until the dust settled. It's not settling. I don't know how they found me."

"Oh, my—You're kidding, right?!" That's when it hit me. "You think I told the press where you were?"

"No." He shook his head. "I don't think that at all."

"You accused me of selling information to the press," I said. Everything was falling into place. "You think this is my fault?"

"No. I found the laptop. It was where you said it was. I know it wasn't you."

"Good to know," I muttered. "If it wasn't me, who was it?"

"I don't know," he replied. "It was just a matter of time."

Roxy meandered toward him and gave him the puppy eyes. She was sympathizing with him. It was cute. But I was still not happy with him. "Whatever," I said. "You've got drama. I don't want anything to do with it."

"Understood."

"I'm going to take a shower," I said and walked out of the room.

I didn't know what to say to him. I was torn between hating him and feeling bad for him.

Chapter Ten

Ethan

I had no right to impose on Ava. She was pissed at me. I had accused her of an atrocious crime. Then accused her of sleeping around. I was an asshole. I was a bigger asshole for using her to save me from my own bullshit.

"I don't know, Roxy," I said and sat down on the couch. The dog hopped up and sat down beside me. "I should go. Your mom is way too nice. She should tell me to fuck off. Pardon my language."

The dog flipped onto her back, legs up and asking for a belly rub. I obliged and mulled over what to do next. After I had a few minutes to think about everything, reality was sinking in. I panicked, and in the heat of the moment, I ran away. It wasn't like that was going to make the problem go away. It was still there. I still had to deal with it.

Ava was a good lady and she helped me out, but I couldn't continue to take advantage of her. I needed to get my shit together and figure it out. I could go to a hotel. It wouldn't take much to have Lucas send me the company card info to use.

"I've got to go," I said to Roxy. "Tell your mom thanks and goodbye for me."

I knew it was the right thing to do. Even though I knew she hated me, I was still ridiculously drawn to her. I wanted her. It would be way too easy to fall into old habits. Even when she was glaring at me, I wanted to grab her and kiss her beautiful face. I might be being a little arrogant, but I had a feeling she would probably be okay with the kissing.

Then we would fall into bed. She would end up with regrets and end up really hating me.

I looked around for a piece of paper to leave her a note. It was a little cowardly, but I didn't want to wait around for her to get out of the shower. It would just end up being another argument. While I was looking for a pen, my phone started ringing. I was positive the press couldn't have gotten my number.

I glanced at the screen and saw it was Lucas. I needed to talk to him, anyway. "Hello," I answered.

"Where are you?"

I looked around the room. There was an accusatory tone to his question. That made me think he was watching me. "Why?"

"I just got a message from one of my contacts in the media," he said. "They know where you are."

"Yeah, it would have been nice to know that thirty minutes ago," I said wryly.

"What do you mean?"

"They were at the rental house I've been staying at," I told him. "They got some shots of me looking like an idiot."

"Shit," he muttered. "What happened? Are they still out there?"

"I don't know," I said. "I left."

"I assume they followed you," he said.

"No. Not exactly."

"Why do I sense there is something I'm not going to like?" he asked with a sigh. "Please tell me you didn't hit anyone."

"I didn't hit anyone. I escaped out the back door and ran. I left my wallet in the house. I called the only person I know here."

"Shit," he groaned. "You called Ava?"

"I did."

"Where are you?" he asked.

"I'm at her apartment," I said. "I was just going to call you, actually. I need some money. I'll go to a hotel."

He was quiet for several seconds. "I can't believe I'm going to say this, but will she let you stay there?"

"Are you serious?"

"If you go to a hotel, someone on the staff is going to give up your location," he said. "I would say hop on a plane and come home, but I don't think that's a good idea. Shit is blowing up. If you can lay low for a few days, it would be for the best."

"Why are they here?" I asked. "What happened now?"

"Someone leaked information about the case," he said. "Apparently, according to this anonymous person, Collin is going to be charged with distribution and manslaughter."

My stomach dropped. "Is there any legitimacy to the rumor?"

His hesitation confirmed my biggest fear. "Yes," he said. "Collin's lawyer talked to your parents and told them to prepare for the worst."

"Fuck," I hissed.

"The national news picked up the story, which is why the press there in Hawaii is jumping on it," he said. "We knew this was coming."

"I didn't think it would actually happen," I said. "Now what?"

"I'll get a call into the PR team," he answered. "I think at this point the only thing you can do is hide."

"So brave," I murmured.

"I know it sucks," he said. "The mob here is bad. I'm sure your mother will be calling soon."

"I'm sure she'll just have an extra glass of wine and sleep through it," I said.

"Are you going back to the rental?" he asked.

I rubbed a hand over my face. "I don't know. I think I should probably stay away. I don't know how serious these people are. If there is actually a manslaughter charge, someone might camp out."

"Would she go for you?" he asked.

"No." I shook my head. "I mean, she would, but I'm not sending her over there to get my things. That'll connect her to me and then she's involved. You said we need to keep her far from this."

"Good point," he said. "I guess you're going to be doing some internet shopping."

"Yeah, fun fact, I'm in Hawaii. There's no overnight delivery."

"Shit," he said. "You know how to pick the right place to hide."

"I'll figure something out," I said. "Just keep me in the loop. I don't want to talk to my parents. I'm going to put the phone on silent and pretend I'm someone else."

"Sounds good."

I wasn't going anywhere. Now, I just had to convince Ava to let me crash for a day, maybe two. I felt hunted. I couldn't seem to find a deep enough hole to hide in. I flopped down on the couch and tried to figure out my next move.

There was a knock at the door. My eyes widened. Roxy and I looked at each other at the same time. She was waiting for me to react. I was waiting for her to do something. She was the dog after all. I was going to go with the not moving thing. We would stay perfectly still, and the person would go away. Someone knocked again. Roxy hopped off the couch and barked a couple of times.

I rushed down the short hall to Ava's room. "Ava?" I whispered and knocked.

She didn't answer.

"Ava," I hissed louder. Roxy barked again.

I pushed open the bedroom door and caught her pulling on a pair of shorts. She was wearing only a bra and panties. My breath caught.

"What are you doing here?" she gasped and pulled the shorts up. "Get out!"

"Someone is at the door," I said and gave her my back. "The press—"

"Oh, hell no," she growled. "Those assholes will not knock on my door."

"I'm sorry," I said. "I didn't think they followed us."

She shoved at my back. "Move." She walked out and then stopped. "Stay."

I had never felt more like a dog than I did in that moment. I closed the door, leaving it open a crack so I could hear what was happening. "Down, Roxy," Ava ordered.

I heard the front door open. "Hello, Mahala," I heard her say. I relaxed a little.

I listened to the two women talk for a minute. The door closed. "You're fine," Ava called out.

I walked out of the bedroom. "Everything okay?" I asked.

"It was just my neighbor bringing me back some of my dishes," she said. "Relax."

"Sorry," I muttered. "It just seemed a little odd."

"Newsflash, I have friends," she said dryly. "They come over. That's what normal people do."

"I get it."

She stared at me with her wet hair hanging down her back. "So, what now?" she asked. "Do you have a plan? I won't bother asking you what is going on because it's pretty clear you aren't going to tell me. But I think I should get to know what the plan is moving forward."

"I don't have a plan," I said. "I have no idea what I'm doing."

She let out a long breath. "Do you want some coffee? Soda?"

"A soda would be great," I said.

She tossed a can of generic soda at me. I waited a few seconds before opening it. "Thanks."

"Tell me what happened," she said and sat down at the table.

I was glad she wasn't throwing me out just yet. I knew that day was coming. I was hoping to put it off as long as possible. "I was at the house. I had gotten up earlier and went for a run. Got home, showered, ate, and then did some work. I was feeling a little stir-crazy and decided to go for a hike. I grabbed my keys and phone, not realizing in the moment I had forgotten my wallet. I opened the front door and was hit with a barrage of flashes and shouted questions. I didn't know what was happening. And then I did. I rushed back inside and panicked."

"They were shouting questions at you?" she asked.

"Yes. I didn't think I could stay there. I ran out the back door. I snuck around the bushes and ran down that road behind the house. I was going to call a ride and go to a hotel when I realized my wallet was at the house."

She nodded as I talked. "And that's when you called me."

"I know I had no right to call you, but I was in a tight spot," I said.

"And you think they are going to go away?" she asked.

"I honestly don't know," I answered. "I don't know. I have no idea what to do. I'm out of my depth. Usually, I would have security. I'm on my own out here and now I don't have my wallet. My credit cards. My laptop."

She rolled her eyes. "You want me to go to the house for you. I'll get your wallet and pack your shit and then drop you off at a hotel."

I had no right to ask her for anything. "I don't think that's a good idea."

"Why?"

"Because if the press is there, they are going to hound you," I said. "They might find out who you are and end up at your front door. They are going to want to know your connection to me. It's not going to be good for you."

She was glaring at me. "What did you get me involved in?"

"Is the house in your name?" I asked.

"It's in my LLC's name," she replied. "Why?"

"Because they will look up property records."

Her mouth dropped open. "Are you serious?"

"It's happened before," I said. "These so-called journalists are more effective detectives than actual detectives. It's why I had to charter a plane here. I knew they would track my private plane. I put the charter under another name."

"If you don't have your wallet or your clothes, what's your plan?" she asked.

I cringed. "I don't know."

She blew out a long breath. "I suppose that means I'm stuck with you."

"Please," I said. "I'll sleep on the couch. I'll stay out of your way. I can Venmo you money."

"This is so not fair," she said.

"I know," I agreed. "I'm sorry."

Chapter Eleven

Ava

It was just a little strange to be shopping for a man who was not my dad. I had attempted to go to the house and get some of Ethan's things only to find out the press was staking it out. I definitely did not want to have them following me. Ethan needed clothes. He couldn't keep wearing the same shorts and T-shirt. We weren't exactly the same size.

I picked up a shirt from the rack, checked the tag, and tossed it in the cart. I doubted Ethan had ever worn anything from Wal-Mart in his entire life. He could complain all he wanted, but if I was the one doing the shopping, he was getting Wal-Mart clothes. I had picked up an extra shift at the coffee shop and been dealing with my rentals. I didn't have time to hunt down designer anything.

I tossed in some underwear and a couple of pairs of shorts. After picking up some toiletries, I headed for the grocery area and grabbed some groceries. Most importantly, I loaded up on beer. I spent more than I had ever spent for myself in one setting. It was courtesy of Ethan. He sent a thousand dollars to my Venmo account. He said it was less than what he would pay for a hotel to make me feel a little better about taking the money.

I had not lived with anyone since my father. I had come to the realization I didn't like living with anyone, especially not arrogant neat freaks. The guy was anal. If I left a shoe in the wrong spot, he moved it. He was constantly cleaning the kitchen and dusting the living room. I wasn't a slob, but he made me feel like one. He insisted on cooking large meals. I knew he was bored, but he was driving me fucking bananas.

Ethan complained about everything. He was pissed about the situation and wasn't doing a great job of keeping it to himself. He was still not telling me what happened. I didn't live under a rock and had seen his picture on the newspapers. I didn't do a lot of anything on the internet. I supposed part of me didn't want to look. I didn't want to know what he had done. There was a part of me that still wanted to believe the best about him. I still had feelings for him. The damn things wouldn't go away.

Those feelings usually reared their ugly heads when I was in bed at night. I could feel his presence. He was on the couch, but it was like he was in bed with me. I could smell him. Hear his breathing. The apartment was not big enough for the both of us. Not big enough for us to have our own space. He was everywhere. I woke in the morning and he would already be awake sipping coffee.

And there was the fact he had pretty much confiscated my dog. Roxy had taken to sleeping with him. Last night I had gotten up and found Roxy curled up against him on the couch. He couldn't have been comfortable, but he never said a word. He was sexy as hell. It had taken everything I had not to ravage him. I had gone back to bed, but I didn't sleep a wink. I kept running different scenarios through my head. Even now, I couldn't stop the fantasies.

A hand caressed over my arm, immediately waking me. I open my eyes and could only see a shadowy figure. He leaned down and let me see his face. It was wrong. It was wrong to want him to climb over me. I shouldn't want to touch him. Instead, I kissed him. He kissed me back and crawled over me. The weight of his heavy body pressed me against the mattress.

"Dammit," I slapped at the steering wheel.

It wouldn't stop. It was in a loop running through my head. The fantasies my brain conjured were pretty outrageous. I was willing him to sneak into my room and take me. I would protest just enough to preserve my dignity. After the deed was done, I would kick him out of my bed. I would get to scratch the itch and then maybe I could forget he was around. That wouldn't happen, but I could at least get rid of the fantasies. I'd been walking around the last couple of days with my panties wet. I wondered if he was feeling anything. Was he even a little attracted to me?

I got home and almost dreaded going inside. I was trying to avoid him. Unfortunately, I couldn't stay away from my own house forever. I carried in the first group of bags. Ethan was sitting at the table with my laptop, something he was doing a lot lately. I carried the bags to the table and dropped them.

"Don't worry, I'll get the rest," I snapped.

"I can't really go outside."

"Of course, not," I said.

I stomped back out to the car and grabbed another load of bags. He was still sitting at the table when I walked in. I dropped them on the table, nearly knocking over his bottle of water. He looked up at me with an expression that made me want to knock it from his face. I kept my cool and went out for the last bags.

When I returned, he closed the laptop and started to sort through the bags. Together, we put away the groceries. It was a little strange to work with him like we had done it a hundred times before.

"I didn't know what to get," I told him when he pulled out one of the T-shirts.

"It's good," he said. "Thank you. I appreciate you doing this for me. I'm sorry I'm a burden on you."

"Whatever," I murmured.

"I'm going to change," he said and took a bag of the clothes.

I grabbed a beer. It was a little warm from the ride home, but I didn't care. I sucked down the beer and contemplated what to do next. I could not spend the next few hours trapped in the apartment with him. He took up so much space. Not physically, but just him. His personality was huge. He just took up so much space!

He came back into the room wearing the new clothes. I reached out and pulled the sticker from the front of the shirt indicating the size. "Good as new," I said. "Want to know how much that shirt cost?" I teased.

"I don't care."

"Ten bucks." I grinned. "I bet you don't even wear socks that cost ten dollars a pair."

"I don't care, Ava," he said. "I'm just grateful to have something new to put on. Thank you."

Now he was being nice. I couldn't take it anymore. I was going to jump him if I didn't get away from him. "I'm taking Roxy for a walk," I said.

"I'll go with you," he offered.

I raised an eyebrow. "I thought you couldn't leave the house," I said.

He pulled out the baseball cap I bought, along with the sunglasses. He put them on and then rubbed his jaw covered in thick stubble. "I'm in disguise."

I supposed the generic tennis shoes and clothing along with the sunglasses and unshaven look did change his appearance. He certainly didn't look like the man who'd showed up to the rental house the first day.

"Okay." I shrugged. "If you think you're ready. Just know if you get spotted, I won't be sticking around waiting for you. I'm out."

He smirked. "Good to know."

"Every man for himself," I joked.

"Cutthroat."

I put the leash on Roxy and headed out the front door. Ethan followed me with his disguise on. "Damn, it feels good out here," he said.

We walked toward the beach with him stretching his arms out and inhaling deeply. I imagined it would be tough to be trapped inside. "How long do you think you're going to have to be cooped up?" I asked.

"Lucas said it was still pretty hot," he said. "The moment I pop my head up, the story gets new fuel. I need to hide out a little longer. I know I'm a pain in the ass. I'm sorry. But thank you for being so generous. I do want to repay you."

"You've already paid."

"Still," he said. "You've done a lot."

"Does this have anything to do with your brother?" I asked him.

"You really haven't looked it up?"

"No," I said. "I don't want to know."

"Yes," he confessed.

"Yes, what?"

"Yes, it has to do with my brother," he said. "My brother has made a lot of mistakes in his life," he explained. "He just keeps making them. I don't think he's ever going to grow up. He shows no remorse. He's a one-man wrecking ball. He's spoiled and entitled. He's got an endless supply of money."

I could empathize. "I get it," I said. "My sister is the same way. She called me."

"Recently?"

"Yes." I sighed. "We haven't talked in a long time and she calls me asking for help. She's in trouble. I don't know what she thinks I'm going to do for her. She keeps getting herself into hot water and expecting everyone to fix it for her. Now that our parents are gone, she doesn't have anyone. I swear she actively seeks out trouble."

"She and my brother would get along well," he joked.

"The two of them together would be dangerous." I laughed. "I hope they never meet. Then again, there are so many just like them it doesn't matter."

"I guess we're both hiding in Hawaii from our younger siblings," he said. "At least your sister's drama isn't following you."

"No, not anymore," I said. "It did when I was there. It was why I had to leave. Nothing seemed to stop her. When I was in college, she got into trouble. She was fourteen. Of course, she was saved from actually facing any consequences."

"Sounds exactly like my brother," he said.

"It must be the youngest sibling thing," I agreed. "Or do you have other siblings?"

"No," he replied. "Just me and my brother. We used to be really close. He was always tagging along with me and my friends. I blame myself sometimes because I introduced him to things I was doing when he was not old enough to deal with it. He played with the big boys. He liked what he saw, and despite being twelve or thirteen, he kept doing it. Except after I went into the military, I wasn't there to look out for him. He started getting into a lot of trouble."

"Like partying?"

"Partying." He nodded. "Drinking. Drugs. Skipping school. He just went wild. I don't know if my parents didn't notice or if they assumed it would get better eventually. My mom used to say he was going through a phase. He got into enough trouble he needed to go to rehab a couple of times to avoid being thrown in jail. It just never sank in. About a year into my Navy career, I got a call from my dad that he had overdosed. It was a close call. I thought for sure that would be enough to send him a wake-up call. It wasn't. He paused his partying, but it didn't last for long."

"I'm sorry," I said with genuine empathy. I completely understood what he was going through. "I was never all that close to my sister. When we were really little, yes, but as I got older, I started to resent my mother and the life she forced us into. My sister embraced it. She couldn't get enough of it. She and my mom were very close. As close as two shallow people could be."

We talked and walked until it was long past dark and time to get home and make dinner. It was nice to actually have someone who could relate to my family drama.

Chapter Twelve

Ethan

I was going out of my mind. I was not used to being so confined. Even though I spent long hours at work back in New York, I knew I had the freedom to leave. I was stuck. I had never been in jail, but I imagined it was a similar feeling. The press were my guards. They were still swarming. Ava had a run-in with them at the coffee shop. Thankfully, they didn't know who she was. They were asking everyone if they had seen me.

I would never understand how they could stalk people and get away with it. It was still stalking. I didn't care if it was all in the name of writing a story. It wasn't like they were interested in facts. They were writing nonsense. It was all fairytales. I knew they were bullshit stories, but no one else did. People actually believed them. Ava insisted she wasn't reading the internet, but I wasn't sure I believed her.

Then again, if she had read the stories, she would know who I was. If she found out who my family was, she was going to kick me out on my ass. She wouldn't let me crash on her couch. She'd be the first one to call the media and send them directly to me.

"Roxy, are you bored?" I asked the dog asleep at my feet. "How do you do this every day. I'm so ready to get out of here. I was not made for this life. Maybe that's why I'm not like my brother. I would never be able to go to jail. Or prison. I don't break the law because I don't want to be in prison. Collin never learned that lesson."

"Talking to the dog again?" Ava asked as she walked through the door.

"She's a pretty good listener," I replied. "I think that means I've officially crossed into Crazy Land. I made protein balls."

She laughed. "You really are bored."

"I was bored last week. Today, I'm out of my fucking mind."

"You need to get out of here," she said.

"Yeah, no kidding, but I don't see that happening anytime soon," I told her. "Lucas said my house in New York has been staked out. My parents are talking about going to London for a couple of months. I hate the idea of running or hiding, but I certainly don't want to spend my life living on the front page of every gossip rag in the country."

"You have to get out of here," she reiterated.

I looked up at her. She was kicking me out. The time had come. "I see."

"Why don't you go put on those cute little swim trunks," she said. "I know a fairly private beach. It's time to practice your surfing skills."

Just the idea of getting out of the apartment appealed to me. "Okay."

I hopped off the couch and grabbed the ugly swim trunks she had bought for me. They were pink with dark pink flamingoes on them. I was pretty sure she bought them to be cruel. The joke was on her because I didn't care. The idea was to be incognito. The shorts were not something I would ever wear in my normal life. They were ugly as sin, but I didn't care. If it meant I got to be outside, I was willing to do it.

I returned to the living room and waited. She came out wearing her cutoff jean shorts and a loose tank. I was looking forward to seeing her in her swimsuit again. That was reason enough to risk giving away my location.

She drove us to a place that was definitely out of the way. I was nervous. The last thing I wanted to do was get seen. But I had to get out of that apartment. There was a guy waiting on the beach. He waved at Ava.

"Thank you!" She gave the man a hug. "I appreciate this. I owe you one."

She thrust one of the boards at me. "Let's go," she said. "There's nowhere to rent boards here," she explained. "I figured it would be a lot easier to just borrow a couple of boards."

She stripped down to her bathing suit once again. I pulled off my shirt and carried the board out to the water. I felt a little more confident now that I had gotten a little time on the board. We paddled out and floated on the water, waiting for the chance to get up and actually ride a wave.

"There's one coming in," Ava called out.

I looked out and saw it. I remembered everything she taught me. My confidence was much higher than it had been. I got up, arms out, and rode the wave. I rode it all the way to the shoreline. I hopped off and held up my arms in triumph.

"I did it!" I exclaimed. She laughed and joined me at the water's edge.

"You killed it," she said. "I think you just might be ready for the North Shore."

"Yeah, I'm not quite ready to die," I joked. "I'll stay on the bunny slopes."

"Soon," she said. "You're a natural."

After a few more runs, we headed for the beach and laid out directly on the warm sand. This was what I had expected from my time in Hawaii. "Damn," I breathed. "I feel so much better."

"You were getting a little pasty," she teased. "You needed to get your ass out of that apartment. You were starting to funk up the place."

"Funk up?" I questioned. "Are you saying I stink?"

"I'm saying you don't smell like you used to."

"Maybe because I don't have access to my usual products and cologne," I said. "What is that shit you bought me?"

"I don't know." She shrugged. "My dad always wore it. It's not like I buy a lot of men's products."

"Great, you made me smell like your dad," I groaned.

"You definitely don't smell like my dad," she said with a laugh. "You have your very own unique scent."

"Okay, I'm not sure if you're offending me or complimenting me."

"Maybe both," she joked.

"I really do appreciate you shopping for me," I said. "I don't want to sound ungrateful."

"I think you're being a good sport about all of it," she replied. "I don't know a lot of guys who are like you that would be able to settle for cheap stuff."

"It's not so bad," I said. "I miss my freedom. Unfortunately, if I expose myself, I'm still not going to be free. They will hound me. I won't be able to do anything, go anywhere, or even eat a meal."

"Do you think it will end soon?" she asked. "I thought these scandals were usually over in a week or so."

"Usually, but it's a slow news cycle apparently," I muttered. "Not to mention, people my brother has messed with in the past are all taking advantage of the situation. They all want their fifteen minutes. A hooker just came forward to add her two cents to the story."

"I'm sorry," she said. "I don't like you, but I don't want you to suffer."

I laughed at her statement. "I'm not sure that was a compliment."

"It's not supposed to be. It's just the facts."

"Understood." I nodded.

She said she didn't like me, but I had a feeling she liked me a little. If she didn't like me, she would have hung me out to dry. "I hope you know I'm not trying to take advantage of you. I know it probably seems like that, but I swear, I'm so grateful for your help. I wish you would let me pay you."

"I don't need you to pay me," she said.

"I was thinking about a plan to get back to the house," I said. "If you let me borrow your car, I could sneak in through the back. I'll leave my rental out front and they'll never know the difference. I can get my laptop and stuff. I'll call the car guy and have him come and pick it up."

"Does that mean you're going home?" she asked softly.

"I don't know," I said. "I can't keep hiding in your apartment. I can't go home. I don't really know what I'm going to do, but I want to feel whole. If I have all my shit, I'll be in a much better position to get up and go if I need to."

"Good idea," she said.

"I'm not sure I can, so please don't throw me out just yet," I said.

"We'll see. I think I might have to keep your security deposit."

"Hey, why?" I asked.

"You're right," she said. "We all know you're a total neat freak."

"I'm not a neat freak," I protested.

"Oh, my goodness," she groaned. "You rearranged my pantry! All my cans are organized by fruits and vegetables. You faced them all forward. You're a freak."

"I promise you, that's not my usual thing," I told her. "I just get a little bored. I was looking for a can of soup and I couldn't find the one I wanted. Then I went down a rabbit hole."

"It was a little creepy," she said. "Ever seen that Julia Roberts movie? That's what it looked like."

"I hear you," I nodded. "I'll go mess it all up."

"Nah, I kind of like it," she said with a laugh. "It does make it a lot easier to find things."

"I figured you would prefer I attacked the pantry and not your panty drawer," I teased.

She laughed it off. I wanted to stay on the beach forever. The stress that had been building over the last week was slowly fading away. It was the best medicine. We stretched out on the beach until the sun started to set.

"Do we have to?" I groaned.

Ava was up and pulling on her clothes. "Roxy is going to want dinner. I want dinner."

"I was thinking I could make those BLTs I told you about yesterday," I offered.

"You're making me feel like I should be paying you for all the cooking and cleaning you've been doing."

"I'm just trying to earn my keep," I said. "I don't want you to throw me out on my ass."

"We'll see how these BLTs go. Then we'll talk."

"Trust me, you're never going to want another sandwich again," I said. "I'm not a great cook, but I can make bacon."

"I don't think bacon is exactly rocket science." She laughed.

We returned the boards and headed for her car. "I think I might actually be able to sleep tonight," I said.

"I'll have to start walking you like I walk Roxy," she said.

"Please do," I replied. "I need it."

"For your sake, I hope it ends soon," she continued. "I hope my sister never puts me in the position your brother put you in. I'm not sure I could handle it as well as you are."

"I don't think I'm handling it at all," I admitted. "I swear I found a gray hair this morning. All this sitting around and hiding is stressing me out."

She looked over and offered me a comforting smile. It helped. The whole situation could be a hundred times worse. She made it tolerable. And I was pretty sure she didn't hate me as much as she did when I started sleeping on her couch. That was progress.

Chapter Thirteen

Ava

"Good boy, Ruger," I said to the dog. "I'll see you later."

I delivered him to his house and walked back to my car. It was one of those days. A typical day, but it just felt like my plate was full. It was the coffee shop, then the dogs, and now it was off to the condo. I was glad it was rented for the week. I needed to make sure it was all neat and tidy and ready for tenants. I put the pineapple on the kitchen counter and made sure the house rules were front and center. I tapped the air freshener in the bathroom and fluffed the pillows on the couch.

Satisfied the place was ready for guests, I left and made my way to the apartment. I had to put the new sheets on the bed before renters came in tomorrow. After the disgusting party animals, I opted to throw away the bedding. Washing it just didn't feel like enough. I bleached and wiped down the counters once again. I could smell the cleaning products. I would normally leave a couple of windows open, but there was a storm coming in and I didn't want to deal with wet floors.

By the time I got home, I was ready to kick back and relax. To my surprise, Ethan and Roxy were sitting on the stoop. He had his so-called disguise on. A pink box was sitting next to him.

"What are you two doing out here?" I asked.

"Getting some fresh air and watching the storm clouds roll in," he answered.

I pointed to the box. "And what's that?"

"Oh, just a little something special." He grinned.

He picked up the box and opened it. My eyes practically popped out of my head and my mouth watered at the sight of my favorite donuts. They were my absolute favorite treat. I didn't get them often because they were so rich and delicious and just a little expensive. They were my guilty pleasure.

"You didn't," I breathed.

"Oh, I did." He nodded.

"How did you know?" I asked.

"I remembered you saying you hadn't had one in a while," he said with a shrug. "Roxy and I went for a walk and I saw the bakery. I know you had a long day today. I thought you could use a little treat."

"That is so nice." I smiled.

He scooted over and made room for me on the stoop. I helped myself to one of the coconut-filled treats. I took the first bite and moaned. "So good."

He snatched one from the box. "They are addicting," he said around a mouthful. "I don't think I've ever ate two donuts in one sitting. I can feel my blood sugar spiking."

I laughed and wiped my mouth. "They are so sweet and so good. So fresh."

"There was a line out the door," he said. "I took that as a good sign."

"Always." I nodded. "It's always packed. It's another reason I don't go very often. I never have time to stand in that line."

"It wasn't bad," he said. "And Roxy was a perfect lady. I may have gotten her a little treat."

"Oh really." I smiled. "Did you get a treat, Roxy?"

She was sitting next to Ethan looking very satisfied. I was a little jealous of their relationship. She had really taken to him. I was a little worried she was going to end up liking him more than me. But he was going to be going home soon. Then it would be just me and her. Again. All alone.

While we were sitting there, the neighbor who lived a couple doors down just happened to walk outside. I saw her watching us. She was pretending to sweep the sidewalk, but her attention was on us.

I smiled and waved. "Hello!"

"I should go inside," Ethan said in a low voice.

With the way my neighbor was staring, I got it. She was just a little too interested in what we were doing. There was no reason for her to be staring. It was pretty rude. Ethan walked inside with Roxy. I didn't want to look like we were hiding and stayed seated. The woman was the only one of my neighbors I didn't really get along with. She was always complaining about something. If kids were playing the front area, she would sit out in her chair and glare at them. She was always looking for a reason to yell at them. She was nosy. We all knew it and tolerated her.

The neighbor walked over. "Did you get a roommate?" she asked.

"No."

"I've noticed that man has been around a lot the last week or so," she commented. "Is he your brother?"

"I don't have a brother," I replied without getting up.

"He doesn't leave the house much," she said.

I said nothing. It was a little disturbing to have someone watching me and my house so close.

"Is he your boyfriend?"

"No," I answered.

I could feel her frustration growing. She was pissed I wasn't giving her the information she felt she should have. It was a little satisfying. I had a secret and she didn't know it. It must be killing her. She was so used to knowing everything about everyone in the neighborhood. She used her knowledge for power. She manipulated people to do what she wanted. Either they caved or she used her information to threaten them. In some circles, that would be called blackmail.

"Isn't your unit a one-bedroom?" she asked.

"It's exactly like yours," I replied.

"One bedroom," she confirmed with a slow nod. "So, he is your boyfriend?"

"Is there a reason you think you need to know?" I asked and got to my feet. I was not going to keep sitting down and let her spew her nonsense. The woman was short and round. She spent her days spying. I felt bad for her. I knew she was a lonely old woman with no family and few friends. I had a feeling her lack of friends was due to her personality. She was obnoxious. I tried so hard to be nice to her. I used to take her treats and offered to help her with anything she needed. My goodwill had been rejected and twisted into something sinister and I wasn't a glutton for punishment.

"I live here," she said haughtily. "I have a right to know who my neighbors are. I don't know him. The way he skulks around and always wears those dark sunglasses is very suspicious. I fear for my safety."

"Trust me, you're safe," I told her. "He's not going to skulk over and harass you."

"Does the landlord know about this man living in your home?" she asked. "We're not supposed to have guests for more than three days. I've seen him there for more than a week."

"I think you should probably mind your own business," I said. "Honestly, he's not hurting you. He's not making trouble. It's not like we're throwing wild parties every night. You wouldn't even know he was here if you weren't stalking me."

"I'm a concerned citizen," she countered.

"I think your concern is misplaced," I replied. "I'm not shacking up with a criminal. Trust me, your body is very safe from him."

"What's his name?"

"Why in the world do you think I would ever tell you that?" I asked incredulously. "You need to check yourself. You're not my landlord. You're a neighbor. I've tried to be kind and patient with you, but you're pushing me."

She gave me a dirty look. "I suppose I could just let the landlord know you've allowed someone to move in with you," she sneered. "Then you'll have to tell him who the man is. I want him to have a background check."

"And I want a million dollars. I think we're both going to walk away disappointed."

"How dare you be so flippant about this situation," she snapped with her hand pressed against her chest. "I'm a single woman living alone. I deserve to feel safe in my own home. Everyone has been vetted except your guest."

I was about to lay into her when Ethan stepped out. "Everything okay?" he asked.

"Everything is fine," I remarked irritably. "My lovely neighbor here is very concerned you might be an ax murderer who's going to sneak over and attack her in the middle of the day."

He smirked. "I don't think we've met," he said with a smile. "But I can assure you I don't wield an ax in any capacity."

"Why are you here?" my neighbor asked. "Don't you have a home? Are you homeless? Are you just out of jail?"

She was being ridiculous. I expected Ethan to lay into her, and that was only going to make things worse.

"I'm not homeless," Ethan said. "Quite the opposite. I actually own a couple of homes. I have never been to jail, but I have driven by one. I don't think that counts."

"You're not from here," she said.

"No, I'm not." He smiled.

"Who are you?" she asked. I was surprised she was so pushy with him. I understood why she was like that with me, but not with him. She didn't know him. She didn't know what kind of person he was and was being pretty damn bold.

"I'm the man in love with this beautiful woman," he said. "I couldn't stand to be away from her. We're working out our future together."

He grabbed me, and to my surprise, kissed me. His lips pressed against mine with his arm wrapped around my waist in a tight vise. I heard a snort but ignored it. His kiss blocked out everything else.

"Disgusting," I heard the neighbor say before she stomped away.

He made no move to break the kiss. It was too good to stop. My hands slid up his back and into his hair. A gust of wind lifted my hair. He pulled away with a smile on his face. I was left a little shaken and breathless.

"What was that for?" I asked.

"Made her walk away," he replied with a grin.

"Very true." I nodded.

"I noticed her peeking at me earlier. I didn't realize she was that nosy. I guess I'll have to limit my time outside."

"I'm sorry," I muttered. "She's obnoxious. There's always one in the neighborhood."

We went into the apartment and closed the door. I was feeling shaky. I couldn't believe he kissed me. I couldn't believe I liked it as much as I did. He seemed unfazed by the kiss. I didn't know if that was a good or bad thing. I wanted it to be casual, but I wasn't sure I wanted it that casual.

"I need to be more careful," he said. "She's probably taken pictures of me coming and going."

"I'm sorry," I said. "I really didn't think she'd be that nosy."

"It's fine," he replied. "Hopefully, the facial hair and hat will hide who I am. Unfortunately, I have a feeling she's the kind of person who likes to watch a lot of TV and read gossip magazines. I'll need to be careful."

"I'm going to shower," I said.

I had to get away from him before I did something stupid. Like have sex with him. A cold shower was in order.

Chapter Fourteen

Ethan

I couldn't stay in the apartment. Ever since the kiss the night before, I had felt a sense of restlessness that dominated every thought. I wanted her. I wanted her with every cell in my body. Last night had been horrible. I tossed and turned all damn night. The times I did fall asleep, my dreams were way too erotic to be having on someone's couch. I had reverted to teenage boy status.

I did a little work before making my daily call to Lucas. The news was never good. It was always drama and more drama. Talking to him was a lot better than talking to my parents. As long as I was kept apprised of the situation, that's all that mattered. I didn't need the extra theatrics.

"I would love for you tell me the situation went away and I can come home," I said when he answered.

"I wish I could tell you that," he replied.

I could hear the stress in his voice. "What's going on?" I asked.

"There's talks about doing some layoffs," he said. "As you know, we scrapped that deal. We don't have the funds to do it."

"We're not doing any layoffs yet," I said. "I just went over the reports for last month. It's not that bad."

"Next month will be," he said. "You've seen the stock price. Deals we've been working on are on shaky ground. I'm not worried about bankruptcy, but we have to trim the fat."

I rubbed my face. "I assume you've already put together a proposal."

"I have," he said.

"Send it over." I sighed. "I'll take a look at it tonight."

"How's the living situation going?" he asked.

"It's going," I replied vaguely.

I wasn't about to tell him I was having some raunchy thoughts about my landlord. He would send someone to kidnap me and pull me out of the situation. It was none of his business, anyway.

"I know I don't have to say it, but you have to try and keep your distance," he said. "Are you sleeping with her?"

"None of your business."

"You can't get involved with this woman," he said. "Trust me."

"I'm not getting involved," I said. "I'm hiding. She's been kind enough to harbor me. I'm basically a fugitive at this point."

"I know and I'm sorry. I have a proposition for you."

"This should be good," I said dryly.

"I've got an ex who's working in Paris for the next few months," he said. "She asked me to check in on her apartment from time to time. It's a nice penthouse on the Upper East Side. The building is secure and very private. It houses a lot of celebrities. Paparazzi know better than to try and get inside. I can get you in. It has an underground entrance. People use it for clandestine pickups and stuff like that. I know you're still cooped up, but you'll be cooped up inside a penthouse. No one in the building is going to give you shit. The people who live there don't want their business blasted. Leaving the building might prove difficult but we can at least get you back to New York. Eventually, you'll have to come out of hiding. This can't go on forever."

He was right. If I stayed at the apartment, I was going to end up falling into bed with Ava. It was inevitable. We had moved past the stage of her hating me. The kiss proved that.

"Okay," I said. "I'm ready."

"Seriously?" he asked with surprise.

"Yeah," I conceded. "I need to get back to work. My extended vacation has gone on longer than I planned."

"Are you going to go get your things?" he asked.

"Ava offered to go get them," I informed him. "I'll ask her to go soon."

"I'm going to get you a flight today," he said excitedly.

It was moving fast. I knew that was what had to happen. "Okay. Give me a call and let me know the details."

"Looking forward to seeing you again," he said.

"Yeah," I snorted.

I ended the call with him and then sent Ava a text. She was at work and probably wouldn't see it. She had been offering to go get my things, but I had told her not to. It was time. I would be gone before the press could figure anything out. I looked at the dog and realized I was going to miss the girl. And the woman. As hard as it had been to stay cooped up in the apartment, it had been kind of nice. Ava and I had fallen into an easy routine. It was comfortable. It was nice not to spend every evening alone. We had started watching some weird sci-fi show on TV. It had become our routine. I was going to miss it.

"Want to go for a walk?" I asked Roxy.

It was going to be our farewell walk. I clipped the leash on her and was donning my disguise when Ava called. I didn't know why I felt guilty, but I did. "Hey," I answered. "Are you busy?"

"Nope, it's a slow day. What's up?"

"I hate to ask you to do it, but could you go to the house and get my stuff?" I asked. "I could go with you. I'll just sneak around the back."

"No problem," she replied. "I'll swing by after work."

"Thank you," I said. "I hate imposing on you."

"I have to go there anyway," she confessed. "I need to restock the fish feeder."

I cringed again. She was being put out for something she had no involvement in. "Thank you. I'll make it up to you."

"I'm leaving here in a few. I'll go out there and be home in a couple of hours."

"I'm going to take Roxy out for a walk," I said.

"You spoil her," she teased.

"And I love it," I replied. "She's a good girl and deserves it."

"I suppose she does." She laughed. "I'll see you later. It looks like we might get a storm."

"They've said that every day," I muttered.

"This one might actually happen."

"I'll believe it when I see it."

She hung up and Roxy and I set out for our last walk. It did look pretty dreary out. Roxy trotted alongside me. We made it to the beach that was still fairly busy. Obviously, the storm warning wasn't being taken seriously. I was really going to miss the beach. I made a personal vow to go to the beach more often once everything settled. It wouldn't be the same, but I found the beach to be very cathartic. I didn't think I would be able to get through all the bullshit happening in my life if it wasn't for the beauty that surrounded me.

Lucas called while I was walking. "I've got the name of a guy who has a plane on standby," he said.

"Really?"

"Yes," he answered. "He can get you to LA and then we'll get you another flight to New York. I've already set up the payment. You just need to call him and arrange a time. He's on standby."

I got a sick feeling low in my gut. I supposed I wasn't really ready to go. But I had to. I needed to leave before Ava found out who I was and reverted to hating me once again. I wanted to leave on good terms. This seemed like the best way to do that.

"Okay," I said with resignation. "Ava is going to get my stuff. I should be able to be in the air in a few hours."

"Good," he said. "Let's get you home!"

"See you soon." I ended the call.

I slid my phone back into my pocket. I wasn't going to rush back to pack. I supposed I was dragging my feet a little. The wind picked up out of nowhere. The clouds on the horizon seemed to have quadrupled. They were piled up on one another and turning darker by the second. I wasn't going to be able to put off my takeoff.

I called the number Lucas texted. I had to plug one ear to hear the guy. "My colleague called you earlier about getting a flight to LA," I shouted to be heard. "I can be ready in two hours."

"Sorry, man," he said. "The weather service just put out a weather alert. We're grounded."

"What? For how long?"

"It depends on how bad the storm is," he replied. "Maybe tomorrow."

"Tomorrow," I groaned.

"Sorry," he repeated. "I just heard they're delaying and cancelling flights at the airport. It's going to be a good one."

I looked to the sky once again. It did look nasty, but it was still out over the sea in the opposite direction of the mainland. "What if we leave in an hour?" I asked.

"I can't do it," he replied. "If the storm passes by us, then we can do it, but it will be twelve hours before we know."

"Okay," I said. "I guess I'll check back tomorrow."

I didn't know why I was fighting so hard. I didn't really want to leave. But on the other hand, I knew I had to. I had to get my ass out of Ava's apartment. I couldn't hide. She claimed she didn't read the stories, but I wasn't sure that would last for much longer. She had to be curious. Not to mention the nosy neighbor. She was going to put it together soon.

Mother Nature was in charge. The beach started to clear out as the storm got closer. It was kind of exciting. I wasn't ready to concede to the storm just yet. With the beach clearing out, I let Roxy off the leash. I knew she wasn't going to run off on me. She darted in and out of the white surf, hopping and yipping with excitement. I found a stick and tossed it for her. She raced down the beach and brought it back. The wind was whipping around me. Sand pelted my legs and blew against my face. It was getting dark, but I kept my sunglasses on to protect my eyes.

"Let's go, Roxy," I shouted into the wind.

The rain started. It was different than a cold New York rain. It was invigorating. I hooked up the leash and we started on our way back to the apartment. The rain started to pick up. My T-shirt clung to my skin. It was a little cold with the wind blowing over my wet clothing.

I had to take off my sunglasses. It was way too dark. I was glad the pilot had shut me down. I didn't want to be caught in the air during the storm. I didn't have a death wish. We crossed the street just as the sky opened up and poured down, and I started laughing like a crazy person. I was standing in a storm that everyone else had fled nearly an hour ago. I was the only fool still outside. Me and Roxy.

"Come on, girl!" I tugged on Roxy's leash. "We better get home before your mom has my ass for putting you in danger."

She barked and started running. Roxy seemed to be enjoying the weather as much as I was. It was an adrenaline rush. Nothing in my life brought me much excitement. My life was nothing but work and making money. I wore suits all the time. I shaved every morning. I never stepped out of the lines. Being in Hawaii had given me a new view on life. It was what I wanted in my life.

Chapter Fifteen

Ava

I felt like I was rummaging through *his* panty drawer. I threw his clothes into the suitcase he left in the room. His suits were zipped in a garment bag which I carefully put on the bed. I would do the cleanup later. For now, I was just packing him up. I wasn't being very neat about it either. I could hear the storm building outside. The driveway would be a muddy mess if I didn't get out soon.

I stuck his laptop and chargers in the suitcase and zipped it up. I wasn't going to mess with the food. If he wanted it, he could come back and get it. I carried the stuff out to the car and rushed back inside with the rain beating down on me. I did a second sweep to make sure I had everything.

That's when it hit me. He was going to be leaving. The house had somehow become his. It was sad to think he wasn't going to be around. We weren't going to be cruising down the highway in the fancy Porsche with the wind blowing through our hair. It was the end of a fast and furious fling.

It was funny to think I had gone from hating him, to being crazy about him, to hating him again. Now, it was a different feeling altogether. It wasn't the crazy infatuation I felt during that one really glorious week. It was something different. It felt very real. It felt comfortable. I was going to miss him when he left, even if he did get on my nerves a bit. But it was never meant to be. We weren't ever going to be anything more than what we were.

I left the house and locked up. I supposed the rain was a good thing. There was no one stalking the house. No one was dumb enough to sit outside and wait with the hopes of getting a single picture of some dude. My curiosity about his troubles in New York was piqued, but not enough to look it up. I was a little worried about what I might find. I liked that I could think of him as the man crashing on my couch and not the man from New York with a lot of baggage.

I took it easy down the driveway. The last thing I wanted to do was slide off or get stuck. I pulled into the driveway at home. I figured he would prefer to wait to get his things out of the car when the rain stopped. I dashed to the door expecting to rush in only to find it locked. I quickly unlocked the door and rushed inside.

"Ethan?" I called out.

He wasn't home. "Roxy?"

I suspected he had taken her for a walk. He probably didn't even realize the storm was rolling in. They happened fast. I told him it was coming in. I understood why he thought it wasn't going to hit. I wondered if I should be worried. I told myself to give him a few minutes before I went out looking for him. I knew the route he usually took.

The door blew open and a very wet Ethan and an even wetter Roxy burst in. He was laughing when he walked in. "Don't move," I said to both of them.

I rushed to the linen closet to get them towels. I tossed one at Ethan before grabbing Roxy. Just when I was about to towel her off, she did the stance. "Watch out!" I warned.

It was too late. Roxy gave a good shake. Water flew off her, soaking me and getting Ethan even wetter. I thought for sure he was going to freak out. He threw his head back and started laughing.

"I'm sorry," I said.

"It's fine," he said and rubbed the towel over his head. "It's my fault. It's my fault she's wet."

"Are you guys okay?" I asked and dropped to my knees to dry Roxy.

"We're fine," he said. He took off his shoes and put them next to the door. "We went down to the beach. I saw the clouds, but I didn't think it was going to hit that fast. The beach cleared out. It was too tempting to leave. I let Roxy off the leash, and she had a blast. We had the whole beach to ourselves. Even when the rain started, it was awesome!"

He looked like a little boy who had been splashing around in mud puddles. His cheeks were red and there was a glint in his eyes. He looked younger than he had when I first met him.

"Roxy looks like she had a good time," I said. "She loves the rain."

"I believe it," he agreed.

"I went to the house and got your things," I told him. "I didn't want to drag your stuff in through the rain."

"That's fine," he said. "Do you mind if I jump in the shower? I know I'm soaked already, but I'm a little cold."

"Go ahead." I waved a hand. "I'll make you a drink to warm you up from the inside. You'll probably want to make it a quick shower. Losing power is pretty normal."

"Got it," he said. "Can I help with Roxy?"

"No, I'm going to towel her off and then spritz her with a spray that keeps her from smelling like wet dog," I stated. "She dries pretty quickly."

"Sorry," he repeated.

"Don't be. Roxy had a good time."

"Me too." He grinned and grabbed one of the plastic bags as he headed to the bathroom.

"Did you have fun?" I asked Roxy. "You look like you had a good time."

She shook again before trotting off to get a drink of water. I looked out the window to check the progress of the storm and grimaced when I saw the sky had turned black. It was going to be one of those storms.

Knowing what was coming, I filled Roxy's water bowl with fresh water. I pulled open the drawer in the kitchen and made sure my flashlights were working. I had candles all around the house already.

Richard called while I was doing my pre-storm checks. "Hey, girl," he greeted. "You ready for this?"

"I am," I answered. "I haven't checked the weather, though. Is it supposed to be bad?"

"Not too bad," he replied. "I don't think we need to board anything up. I can come over and help you secure the lawn furniture."

"I'm okay," I said. "I'll shove them in the shed. How are you?"

"All good," he said back. "We've got plenty of food and water. Do you have food?"

I loved that he took care of me. It was very sweet. I appreciated the help. I was an orphan, but Richard and my dad's other close friends made sure I was taken care of. "I do," I answered. "We're going to be fine. Thank you for checking in on me."

"We?" he asked. "Is that man still there?"

I grimaced when I realized I slipped up. Richard had spotted me out with Ethan the week before. I tried to play it off, but when he confronted me about my relationship, I couldn't lie. I told him Ethan had to crash on my couch for a couple of nights. I knew he didn't believe me. He was just like a dad.

"He is," I answered.

"I'm going to have to meet this man formally," he said. "Your dad would want me to make sure any man you got with knew you had people looking out for you. We can't let anyone take advantage of you."

I smiled. "I appreciate that, but he's not a serious boyfriend. I promise you he's just crashing on the couch. I'm helping a guy out. There is no funny business."

"Alright," he said. "Just make sure he knows he'll be answering to me if he pulls any nonsense."

"I'll make sure he knows." I laughed. "Thank you for checking on me. You take care."

I ended the call and put my phone on the charger. He made me smile. It gave me the warm fuzzies to know I had good people like him looking out for me. He had been more of an uncle or grandparent than my mother's family.

Ethan had put his phone on the side table so I put it on the charger as well. I suspected he had never had to ride out a real storm. He likely lived in a mansion with a backup generator. Ethan didn't strike me as the kind of guy who liked to rough it.

Roxy made herself comfortable in the living room while I made a couple of drinks to ward off the chill. It wasn't often it got cold in Hawaii, but after getting used to a tropical climate, a little chill could feel like the arctic. The wind was howling, and the rain beat against the window. I searched the fridge and freezer for something to eat for dinner. I grabbed a frozen pizza and popped it in the oven.

Ethan came into the kitchen a few minutes later rubbing his jaw. "I think I've got to trim this back," he said. "I liked it, but now it's driving me crazy."

"I could pick up a trimmer for you tomorrow," I offered.

"Yeah, maybe," he muttered.

"I made you a drink," I told him.

"Ah, thank you," he said and took it in hand. He moved to look out the window. "Damn, it got nasty out there in a hurry."

"That's how it happens," I commented.

"Is this normal?" he asked.

"The weather?"

"Yes, do you get big storms, hurricanes and stuff?" he asked.

"Not really," I answered. "We get normal storms, but that's the beauty of Hawaii, we're not like Florida or the Bahamas. We don't get those nasty storms."

"I'm beginning to understand the appeal to living here," he said.

"We have the occasional earthquake, but otherwise it's pretty mellow," I told him. I wanted to talk up Hawaii. I wanted him to see the appeal and maybe consider moving to the island. That was my own selfish motivation to get him to stay longer. I was beginning to think there might possibly be a relationship budding. We got along well. He was back to being the guy I fell for before he went crazy and accused me of stealing.

"And the volcano thing," he joked.

"Eh, not really," I said. "We should go see one of the dormant ones. I think you would be impressed."

Again, he seemed to avoid the question. He walked away from the window and into the living room to pet Roxy.

"I'm making pizza," I said. "I figure we should probably cook while we have power."

"Do you lose power a lot?" he asked.

"Not a lot, but it happens," I said. "Not as much as it does on some of the smaller islands."

I watched him and tried to think of what I was doing with him. He was stretched out on the floor with Roxy. I couldn't stop thinking about a future with him. I didn't want to get ahead of myself, but the feelings were there. They weren't going away. It was more than sex. We had not had sex which meant it wasn't what was clouding my emotions. It was real. Since he'd been staying with me, it was like dating. We got to know each other and became friends.

I didn't want to fall for him. But that was like shutting the barn door after the horses escaped. It was too late. Now, I was left trying to figure out how I was going to deal with the feelings. He was going to leave soon, and I wasn't sure I would ever see him again. If there was a way to shut this thing down, I would have done it. Letting him crash on my couch had been a mistake. But it wasn't like I could leave the guy hanging. My need to help people had bit me in the ass before.

The oven timer went off, snapping me out of my introspective thinking. I pulled it out and was cutting it when everything went dark. I started laughing. "Perfect timing," I said.

Chapter Sixteen

Ethan

The silence was deafening but it was also extremely loud. The wind and the rain had been obvious before, but now it sounded like it was howling. I got up from the floor and felt my way to the kitchen. A match lit and a moment later, a candle.

"It's fucking dark." I chuckled. "I don't know if I've ever been in such darkness."

"If you've been in New York your whole life, I bet you haven't," she replied.

"It's spooky," I said.

"Are you scared?" she teased.

"I'm intrigued," I replied. "I've been in a couple blackouts, but nothing like this."

"I suppose you have a backup generator," she said.

"I do at my house," I admitted . "My parents do as well. But my penthouse doesn't."

She started laughing. "Your penthouse. Oh, the horror."

"I did have those lights that turned on when the power goes out," I explained. "So, I've never been in total darkness."

"You can take this into the living room," she instructed. "I'll get a couple more going. You won't be in total darkness."

I carried the candle into the living room and lit one of the smelly ones she always ignited when we were watching TV. The small space was lit up with just a few candles. It was actually very romantic.

"Anything I can do?" I asked.

"Nope." She smiled. "Grab some pizza. We're in for a quiet night. No TV."

"I don't mind a bit," I said. "I'm looking forward to it."

We sat down at the table with a single candle burning. The wind continued to howl outside. I was a little worried things might get worse. I wasn't sure I was cut out for a tropical storm.

"Thank you for dinner," I said.

"My pleasure," she replied.

"Is it weird I think this is exciting?" I asked with a laugh. "I mean, as long as there is no real damage and no one is hurt, it's pretty cool. One of the more exciting things to happen in my life."

"I don't think it's weird at all," she replied with a shrug. "This is all pretty normal for us."

We ate in silence for a few minutes while listening to the storm rage outside. "I think I got everything out of the house," she said. "I didn't do a thorough sweep, but I got your laptop and your chargers. It's all in the car."

"Thank you for doing that," I said. "I'm sorry I've been imposing on you so much. You've gone far above and beyond what you needed to. I don't know how else to thank you. I know you're not going to take my money, but if there is anything I can do, please tell me."

"I'm helping out a friend." She smiled.

The candlelight danced across her face, softening her features and highlighting her beauty. "Thank you." I liked that she considered me to be a friend. I hoped she would remember our friendship when she found out who I was.

"Have you heard any more from your family?" she asked.

"Not my family," I answered. "I've been in touch with my friend. He's been keeping me updated about the family. I can't deal with them."

"Are they mad at you?" she asked.

"They're mad at me for not waving my magic wand and fixing the mess," I said. "Or my brother. I don't think they understand they're going after the wrong guy. My brother is at fault. They will never hold him responsible. Even if I could fix this thing, what happens when he does it again?"

"I get it," she said. "You said it was drugs that he's in trouble with?"

It was hard to talk to her about the situation without talking to her about the facts. If only I could tell her all of the details. "Yes," I replied. "He isn't careful when he's high. He's not careful in general, but this time, he screwed up."

"There's going to be legal fallout?" she asked.

"Yes."

"Could you end up in legal trouble?" she questioned.

"No!" I quickly answered. "I was not around when he was doing the drugs. I'm being dragged into it because I've always cleaned up his messes. I'm the one who's always out in front of the situation trying to smooth it over. When there are questions, I have to answer them."

Again, I was glossing over the facts. I couldn't tell her I was the CEO of Mitchell Enterprises. She wasn't prying, she was asking questions as a friend. She was just trying to help. But I had to keep all of that hidden. I turned the conversation to focus on her.

"How about your sister?" I asked. "Have you talked to her?"

"Not since the night she called." She sighed. "I've been thinking about calling her back. I don't hate her, but she drives me crazy. I know what she wants, I'm just not sure I can do it."

"What does she want?" I asked.

"She wants me to offer to save her," she answered. "She probably expects me to buy her a plane ticket and fly her out here to hide."

"I thought you said she had money?"

"She might." Ava shrugged. "My stepfather was bankrolling her addiction, but I'm not sure he still is. I don't talk to the guy. He's kind of an asshole."

"You mentioned you got money from your mother's family. Did she?"

"Yes." She nodded. "We didn't compare notes, but I would guess she got a lot more than I did. She was very close to my mother. I think that sent her into this current downward spiral."

"Can I ask how your mother died?" I asked.

I was probably prying. I didn't mean to, but I was intrigued by her back story. I wanted to know how our families were connected.

"Car accident," she said.

"Ah." I nodded.

"What does that mean?"

"I've been in some family counseling over the years," I said with a chuckle. "In my very unprofessional opinion—" I stopped. "You said your sister and your mother were very close?"

"Yes," she answered. "Two peas in a very rich pod. They went to fashion shows together and worked their magic to get invited to some of the swankiest parties. My mother convinced my stepdad to support my sister. He bought her a car, sent her on lavish vacations, and bought her an apartment in the city. Why?"

"Is your sister still close with your stepdad?"

"I honestly don't know," she answered.

"Okay, back to my very unwanted and unprofessional opinion." I smiled. "Your mom died suddenly. Wait, one more question?"

She burst into laughter. "I think there's a reason you're not a therapist."

"There's probably at least ten reasons I'm not a therapist."

"What was your question?" she asked.

Uh..." I couldn't remember. "Oh! Was your sister partying before your mother died?"

She rolled her eyes. "She was definitely partying before my mother died. I don't know how serious the drug use was, but I know she was doing them."

"Okay." I nodded. "I think the sudden death and loss of your mom shocked her. She turned to the drugs. If your stepdad has pulled back, that probably added to the problems."

"That's very astute," she said with a grin.

"I hope that's a good thing."

"Yes." She nodded. "Both those things are true. I think my mom looked the other way with the drug use because it was mostly prescription meds. Like you were saying about your brother, she was never held accountable. Honestly, I think it's that environment."

"I agree."

"Did you ever experiment with drugs?" she asked.

"Nope." I shook my head. "Not even once. I think Collin scared me straight. I watched him ride that roller coaster and knew I didn't want to be on it. Plus, I was in the military. As soon as I got out, I was thrust into the family business. I was groomed from the day I was born to be the smart one. To be the responsible one. If I got a B at school, my dad was on me. If Collin got a C, they were celebrating the fact he didn't fail. I totally blame my parents. They set him up to fail. They never set him up for success."

"I get it," she agreed. "I totally get that. If I ever have kids, I'm going to be strict."

"Me too." I chuckled. "My kids are going to hate me. I'm going to put GPS trackers in their arms and make them do piss tests once a week."

"Gee, I'm sure that won't cause any problems," she said dryly.

"Fine, I'll just lock them in a room," I said.

"I think I'm going to move my kids to a homestead. I'll homeschool them and shun all worldly things."

"Oh, you're going the Amish route," I joked.

"That's not a terrible idea."

"How many kids do you want?" I asked her.

She wrinkled her nose. "At least two. Maybe three. I want my kids to have built-in friends. When I'm gone from this world, I want them to have each other. I wish I was close to my sister. It would be nice to have a friend in the world."

"And if that one doesn't work out, you want a backup sibling?" I asked.

"Yes." She nodded. "Is that terrible?"

"No." I shook my head. "I wish I had another brother. Or sister. It would be nice to share the burden the other brother puts on us. My parents wouldn't be leaning so heavily on me."

"I would have liked to have had a sibling around when my dad was dying," she said softly. "Someone who could empathize and understand what I was feeling. I had his friends, but they didn't know him the way I did. I don't have anyone who has my shared life experience. I can't sit around on Christmas and reminisce about the way we celebrated when we were younger. It's just me."

I felt guilty for complaining so much about my family. I did have my parents. I was never alone on the holidays unless I wanted to be. They always wished me happy birthday, and even though we weren't close, I had them. She was all alone.

"I get it," I said. "When my brother and I get together on the holidays, it usually ends up in a shouting match. He gets drunk and belligerent and my mother coddles him. My dad gets pissed that my brother is drunk and blames me. They've always made him my responsibility. They are the parents, but they expect me to do all the parenting."

"That's definitely not fair," she stated. "You can't be responsible for him and his choices. Is that what they expect from you with this current situation? They think you're responsible?"

"They think I should have tried to get him to sober up," I answered. "I think I mentioned he was thinking about getting into politics. They have all these people who are supposed to be keeping him on the right path. They failed. Not me. I don't know when I'm going to be able to live my life without him hanging around my neck. It's worse than a ball and chain."

"Alright, my turn for a little unprofessional advice," she said with a smile.

"Hit me with it. We'll call it square. I won't charge you for my services if you don't charge me for yours."

"I think you need to have a serious sit down with your parents," she said. "You have to tell them how you feel. Don't give them any wiggle room. Put your foot down. Tell them you are going to live your life and you have to let your brother do his thing. If he falls, that's on him. Not you. You will not be responsible for him."

"I think I've given them a version of that conversation," I confessed.

"But were you stern?" she asked. "Like really stern."

"Apparently not." I sighed.

"I can't say much about pleasing parents, but I'm a firm believer in living for yourself," she said. "You have to do what makes you happy."

I inhaled. "Thank you. You are the first person who's ever really said that to me. I think I've felt guilty to even think about putting myself first."

"Don't feel guilty," she said. "You deserve it. You get to be happy. You've made the right choices. You should get to reap the rewards. You can't change your brother or fix him. You do you."

Chapter Seventeen

Ava

I didn't want to go to bed. More like I didn't want to go to bed alone. Things were good between us. I felt like we were growing in our relationship. The candlelight was gorgeous. Maybe it was the alcohol. I didn't know. It was the perfect setting. I could only think about one thing.

We were sitting on the couch talking about nothing. I was sitting on his bed. I was going to have to be the one to get up and go to my bedroom. "I should go to bed," I said. "It's late."

"I don't think it's that late," he said. "It feels late because we've been sitting in the dark for hours."

"Sounds like the storm is still raging," he said.

I got up and looked back at him. "Goodnight."

He rose from the couch, bumping into me. "Sorry," he murmured.

"It's fine."

"Ava," he whispered my name.

I knew exactly what he was asking. I leaned in to him and let him take the lead. He kissed me and pulled my body against his. I immediately wrapped my arms around him and hugged him tight. My hands slid up his back, pulling at his shirt. I didn't care what happened beyond the walls. I didn't care if the storm knocked over a hundred trees. I just wanted to be with him.

There was a franticness to the mood. He pulled at my clothes. We stripped naked and fell against each other. His hands caressed my skin, squeezing and massaging. I did the same to him. I couldn't get enough of him. I pulled at his arms and scratched at his back. He grabbed me and lifted me up. My legs wrapped around his waist. He carried me to the bed and lowered me down. His mouth tore away from mine and kissed my chin and over my throat.

His tongue trailed down my throat before sucking my flesh. I groaned and writhed under him. I had longed for his touch for days. A single candle lit the room. The sound of the rain hitting the walls and window in the room felt like music. All of my senses were tuned to him. I liked that there were no lights or even the sound of electricity humming. I focused on his breathing and mine. My hunger for him skyrocketed.

"I need you," I murmured. "Now, please."

His tongue was twirling around my nipple. "You're rushing this."

"It's been too long," I groaned. "Please."

He chuckled low in his throat. The sound vibrated through me. "I feel the same way."

"I've got condoms," I said.

"Where?" he asked with my breast in his mouth.

"Drawer," I moaned and pulled him against me. "Hurry."

"I don't think I'm ready just yet."

"I am," I gasped. "Right now. Ready."

He rolled to the side just a little and slipped his hand between my legs. I was completely unashamed and let my legs fall open. He slipped a finger inside me. I cried out and lifted my hips. He pushed it deeper. I moved my hips, riding his finger until I was crying out with the first orgasm.

"Where are the condoms?" he asked again.

"Drawer," I blindly pointed.

He leaned over and jerked open the nightstand drawer. I watched him tear it open with his teeth and then quickly rolled it on. He was pushing inside me in seconds. I held him close. There was something about him that had me wanting to hold onto for dear life.

"Damn," he breathed against my lips. "I've wanted this."

"Me too."

"I can't get enough of you," he said and pushed up on his arms.

I stared up into his face that was cast in shadows. My hand trailed down his chest and slid around to grab his ass. I pulled him against me. He grunted once. I pulled a second time. "Again," I demanded.

He thrust hard, slapping my headboard against the wall. "Like that?"

"Harder!"

He hit again and again. There was something about him. Sex with him was so different. It was a total body experience. It wasn't just about an orgasm. Every sense was involved. I opened my eyes once again to find him watching me. The determination I saw on his face was intense. He was giving me his all. I reached up and cupped his face. He lowered his mouth to mine once again. I lifted my hips, matching his thrusts one after another.

"You have to let go," he said. "Now, baby. Now!"

The orgasm slammed into me. I let it go. I didn't hold back anything. I didn't care that I was screaming through it. He groaned, shouted, and then cursed with his body going stiff. His head was back with his chin pointing toward the ceiling. I lifted my head and kissed his neck. I sucked at his skin like he had sucked on mine.

He finally fell down on top of me. I could barely drag in a breath. "Damn," I breathed. "Holy shit."

He chuckled and slid away from me. "I was going to say something like that."

I curled up against him. "Sleep in here tonight."

"You're sure?"

"I am very sure," I said. "There's no reason for you to sleep on the couch. Stay with me."

He kissed the top of my head. "I'd like that."

We cuddled together before he went to the bathroom. I got up to blow out the candles before climbing back into bed. He held me close. The wind and the rain no longer mattered. I felt safe in his arms.

"Goodnight," he said.

"Goodnight. I'm sure the power will be back on in the morning."

"I don't care if it ever comes back on," he mumbled, half-asleep already.

I felt the same way. I laid my head on his chest and listened to the steady beating of his heart. It had been a long time since I felt so calm. It wasn't just the sex. It was the experience and being with him in bed. The storm raged around us, and it didn't matter. I let myself think of a future with him. We could make it work. I didn't have to see him day in and day out. If he visited once a month, I was okay with that. I knew I would never cheat on him. Would he be the same?

He was dangerous. My heart was in jeopardy when I was with him. It was way too easy to fall for the man. It wasn't like he even hinted he wanted anything to do with me once he left the island. He had done a good job keeping his distance from me. The sex was a fluke. It was the atmosphere. The candles and the darkness and it just happened. That didn't necessarily mean it was real.

I forced myself to stop thinking about it. There was no point in borrowing trouble. If he got up and left tomorrow, that was it. I couldn't let myself be sad about it. It would be over. Period.

Roxy woke me the next morning with her cold, wet nose nudging my hand. It took me a moment to orientate myself to where I was. The steady breathing beside me told me everything I thought I dreamed was very real. He was still asleep when I got out of bed. I grabbed my robe from the back of the door and quickly pulled it on. I could hear the hum of electricity, and I was a little bummed it was back on. That meant I had to go to work. Our safe little cocoon was no longer.

I quietly closed the door behind me and led Roxy to the back door. "Go potty," I whispered.

I checked the time. I was hoping I could fall back to sleep for a little longer. I wanted to stay with him in bed all day. I grabbed my phone from the kitchen and texted my manager at the coffee shop. I hoped that part of town didn't have power. I was looking for any excuse not to go to work. I didn't dare call in sick. But dammit, I didn't want to go.

She texted me back almost immediately to let me know she was at the shop and everything was fine. "Dammit," I muttered.

I left Roxy in the backyard and crept back into the room. Ethan was sitting up in bed. "There you are," he said.

"Roxy had to go out," I said. "I have to go to work. Feel free to sleep in."

"Power's back?" he asked with a yawn.

"Yep," I nodded. "It wasn't that bad of a storm."

"Is it cool if I go in with you?" he asked.

"You want to go to work with me?" I repeated.

"I've got my laptop back." He shrugged. "I can do a little work. Honestly, I just need to get out of this place. No offense. It's a great apartment but I think I've talked to Roxy more than I've talked to any-one in my life. I'm a little worried I'm losing my mind."

I laughed at his concern. "Then let's do this. I would hate for you to talk Roxy's ear off again."

He threw off the blankets and stalked toward me completely naked. His body was a work of art. I couldn't stop staring at him. "What are you doing?" I asked on a breath.

He tugged at the belt on my robe. "I'm guessing we're in a hurry," he said and pushed it off my shoulders.

"A little bit." I nodded.

"Then we should take a really quick shower together."

I smiled. "We definitely should do that."

The shower took a little longer than it should have but when we got out, we were both feeling pretty damn good.

"I guess when you work at a coffee shop, you don't have to make coffee for yourself in the morning," he stated.

"Nope. Free coffee."

He went out to the car and got his things. "I hope there's somewhere I can plug in the laptop?"

"Yes," I confirmed. "There are plenty of charging stations."

"Perfect," he said. "I'm ready when you are."

I made sure Roxy was filled up with food and water. The fridge seemed to have held up. "I think we should get milk after work," I said. "I'm not sure I want to risk that."

"Agreed. We'll go shopping after work."

"You're suddenly being very bold," I said.

He shrugged. "I think I'm fine as long as I keep on the shades and hat."

I gave him a quick kiss. "Let's roll."

Chapter Eighteen

Ethan

I set up at a table in back. It felt a little strange to be out in the open. I was beginning to think my self-imposed imprisonment might have been a little dramatic. No one knew who I was. They weren't even paying attention to me. Ava had popped over a few times to refill my coffee. She had said the coffee shop was pretty dead due to the storm.

The few people who had come in were focused on their coffee and didn't even look twice at me. They picked up their orders and rushed out. Only one other guy was taking advantage of the free wi-fi in the shop. Feeling hungry, I got up to order a muffin. Ava and her manager, Cindy, were huddled toward the back whispering.

Immediately, my radar was up. Did her manager know who I was? Was she about to call me out? I looked around the shop. It was just me and the other guy. Ava saw me and quickly came up to the counter.

"Hi." She smiled.

"Is everything okay?" I asked.

"Yes, Cindy was just telling me that guy has been in here every day," she said in a low voice. "He comes in and stays almost all day. She's just a little weirded out by it."

I looked over my shoulder. The guy was watching us. When he saw us looking at him, he quickly looked away. It was a little odd, but not anything too crazy. "If she doesn't like it, she should tell him to leave," I said. "Does she want me to?"

"No." Ava shook her head. "It's fine. He's probably a writer or something. She said he's always working on his laptop."

If they weren't worried, I wasn't going to be worried. "Can I get a blueberry muffin and a bottle of water?" I asked.

"Sure."

It felt good to have my wallet back. I felt like a normal human again. After paying for my stuff, I took the muffin and water back to the table. I left it, assuming it would be safe with just one guy in the place. Ava was in the back of the shop. I quickly used the bathroom and checked out my reflection. I barely recognized me. I had to remove the sunglasses inside the shop. I kept the ballcap on and pulled low.

I walked back to my table just as a few customers were walking out of the shop. "Hey," Cindy called me over.

"What's up?"

"Did you have anything on your table?" she asked.

Ava came back up from the back carrying a box loaded with cups and stuff. "What's going on?" she asked.

"I was just asking him if he anything on his table," Cindy explained. I had a couple of customers and didn't notice the guy until he was rushing away from that area. I don't know if he took anything. I didn't see anything in his hand, but he grabbed his stuff and rushed out of here."

I frowned and looked at my computer still sitting on the table. "I didn't have anything important," I said. "Unless he made off with my muffin."

I walked over to the table and looked around. I didn't see anything missing. "All good," I said.

Cindy and Ava joined me at the table. "The guy is a little weird," Cindy said. "He gave me his number this morning. I get so sick of the tourists thinking we're just going to jump in bed with them."

I cleared my throat. Ava started laughing and put her hand on my shoulder. "Not you."

I raised an eyebrow. We both knew that was exactly what she had thought. "Thanks."

I sat down and was about to get back to work when I realized my thumb drive wasn't in the slot. I looked around the table and then under it. "Oh fuck," I groaned. "Son of a bitch."

"Everything okay?" Ava asked.

"No, he took my fucking thumb drive!"

"Are you sure?" Cindy asked. "He couldn't have been over there for more than a second. I was talking to a customer but not for long."

"It's gone," I said. "I had stuff on there. Important stuff."

I was combing through my mental banks trying to think of everything that was on the drive. It was mostly business stuff. Information that was sensitive and was certainly not meant to be in the hands of just anyone.

"Fuck." I rushed out of the coffee shop and looked up and down the street for the guy. I was trying to remember what he'd been wearing. It was a floral shirt, nice and loud. I stared down the sidewalk with only a handful of people and deflated. Everyone was wearing floral shirts.

I walked down one block in the hopes I might see him. He was nowhere to be found. He had snatched my stuff and run. My only question was why? What was he looking for? Why did he target me? Cindy said he'd been in the shop every day. Was he waiting for businessmen to rob? Something didn't feel right. I walked back to the shop that was still empty.

"You have his number?" I asked Cindy.

"Hold on," she said. She put on some gloves and started rummaging through the trash.

"What did he get?" Ava asked worriedly.

"I think just a thumb drive," I said. "It's for my work. I don't think there's any personal information on it, but I can't say for sure. The sensitive business information is bad enough. I don't understand why he targeted me."

"Maybe he thought you were a famous writer." Ava shrugged. "He thought he was stealing a manuscript or something."

"Got it!" Cindy said and waved the paper in the air.

I took the paper and saw the name and phone number. I sat down and quickly typed the name into the search bar. The first hit brought up a reporter linked to a major news outlet. Not the kind of reporter who wrote anything of substance. He was a gossip writer. My heart sank. I knew exactly what he was looking for. While the normal thief wouldn't really understand the information on the drive, he would. He would exploit my company's financial information. He would comb through it and look for any speck of dirt he could twist and turn into something worth reporting.

"What did you find?" Ava asked.

"He's a reporter."

Her face paled. "He's been in here every day."

I nodded. We both knew what that meant. Rather, what it could mean. He might have put together the connection between Ava and me. He was stalking her to get to me. Or he was just hanging out at the shop with the hope I would show up. I was leaning toward the first option. There were a hundred coffee shops. Why would he choose this one? Something wasn't adding up.

"Did he talk to you at all?" I asked her.

She shook her head. "I don't know. I don't even remember serving him. I'm sure I did, but I don't remember."

"Who is he?" Cindy asked.

"A gossip columnist," I said.

"What's he doing in here?" she asked with confusion. "Why did he steal from you? I wonder if he's stolen from anyone else. Great, that's just what we need."

"Did he give away any other information?" I asked. "Did he mention what hotel he was staying at?"

She looked thoughtful. "I didn't really talk to him," she said. "He was a little creepy. Something about him felt wrong."

I looked at Ava. "I have to go," I said. "I need to try and find that guy."

"Wait!" Cindy said. "He had a pen from the hotel around the corner! I commented on it. He left it on the table when he was going to leave. I handed it to him." She told me the name of the hotel.

"I'm going to put my stuff in your car," I said to Ava.

"Where are you going?" she asked.

I stuffed my things into the satchel. "I'm going to get my shit back."

"You can't just walk in there and ask for it?" she asked.

"Sure, I can," I said. "It's mine."

"Do you want me to call the police?" Cindy asked.

"No, I'll handle this," I growled.

"Wait," Ava said. "You can't just go barging in there. You don't want to get into trouble."

"I don't care," I said. "I'll see you later. Unless I'm in jail."

I walked out of the shop and directly to her car. I tossed my stuff into the backseat and started toward the hotel. I knew how to get information out of people. Now that I had my wallet and my money, I would not hesitate to stoop to bribery. I was going to get my shit back, one way or another.

I heard footsteps running up behind me. I immediately went on alert and spun around, prepared to take on whoever was coming at me. It was Ava. "What are you doing?" I asked.

"I'm not letting you do this alone," she said.

"What about work?"

She rolled her eyes. "It's dead. She doesn't need me there. Besides, the next person comes in soon. She feels bad and wants me to help you get your stuff back."

"Thanks."

"What's the plan?" she asked.

"I don't know that I have a plan," I admitted.

She grabbed my arm and pulled me to a stop. "Ethan, take a minute," she said. "I know you're pissed. You have every right to be, but you can't go storming into a hotel. You need to be methodical. You're not going to get anywhere if you don't think."

"I want to kick the guy's ass," I said.

"I know," she agreed. "Me too. Let's get your thing back and then we'll talk about ass kicking. You just told me you've never been in trouble. You don't want to start now. This guy is a snake. Do not let him win by giving him a juicier story."

She was right. "Fine," I said. "I plan on going to the front desk and asking to see him. They'll call up to his room and I'll confront him."

She tapped her finger against her chin. "What if he isn't there?"

"I don't know," I muttered.

"Let's do your thing and I will very casually find a way to see which room he's in," she said.

"Or I could just slip the person a hundred and ask them," I suggested.

She laughed. "That might work. Let's try option one first before we resort to bribery."

I was going to take her word for it. While we were walking, a better idea came to mind. "I want in his room," I said. "I want to know what he has. You know he's hiding out. He's busted. He's like a rat hiding in his hole. I say you tell the front desk you're there to see him. They'll tell him there's a beautiful young woman to see him and is waiting in the lounge. I go up and break in."

"How are you going to break in?"

"Good point," I said.

"Okay, we go back the bribing." She nodded. "Flash a smile if it's a woman. If it's a guy, I'll show some cleavage."

"Works for me," I said. "We'll get him out of the room, get the key, and then I'll toss the room."

"I feel like a spy." She laughed as we started on our way again.

I walked up to the front desk with Ava at my side. It was my good fortune Ava happened to know the young man working behind the desk. She told him some story about the guy stealing her tip jar. Apparently, it was more common than one would think. He was very willing to help. He slipped her a room key and told us the room number, and I slipped him a hundred-dollar bill.

Ava and I waited on the side of a vending machine across from the elevators. As soon we saw the asshole step off the elevator, we rushed behind him and into the elevator. Ava looked up at me and smiled. "I feel like a spy."

"I feel like going back down there and throwing the asshole through a wall."

She took my hand in hers again. "I'm sorry," she said. "This just keeps getting worse for you."

"No. *I'm* sorry," I said. "I hope like hell him being at your coffee shop is just a coincidence."

"I'm sure it is," she assured me. "He's never tried to talk to me."

I hoped she was right. I knew it was time for me to go. I couldn't keep hanging out and waiting for something to happen. It wasn't fair to her.

Chapter Nineteen

Ava

"This one," I said.

I was suddenly very nervous. I looked up and down the hallway to make sure no one was watching.

"Relax," Ethan said. "We have a key. No one is going to suspect anything."

"You're right," I nodded. "Okay."

He put the key in the lock. The light turned green and it was game on. I felt like we should have been wearing gloves. Wasn't that what spies did? The room was relatively neat. There was a laptop sitting on the bed, along with some empty takeout boxes. I went for the laptop first.

"What if he has it in his pocket?" I asked.

"Look in the bathroom," he said and started opening drawers.

I wasn't sure why it would be in the bathroom, but I looked anyway. I opened a couple of drawers and lifted the towels. I didn't see anything. When I returned to the room, Ethan was on the floor looking under the bed. I was beginning to think we were looking for a needle in a haystack. How in the world were we supposed to find a little drive? It was more than likely in his pocket.

"Did he have a briefcase or anything like that when he walked out?" Ethan asked from the floor.

"I didn't really look," I said. "But I don't think so."

"Son of a bitch," he growled and got up from the floor. He had his hands on his hips and scanned the room.

I pulled his suitcase from the closet and started pulling things out. Every article of clothing I pulled out, he picked up and shook it out. Once we searched through all the clothes, I started checking the lining of the suitcase. I unzipped every pocket and hoped it would just magically appear.

"I don't know," I said. "He has to have it on him."

"Fucker," Ethan snapped. "I'm so sick of this shit."

"Should we call the police?" I asked. "He did steal from you."

"Do we know that for sure?" he countered. "We have nothing. Cindy saw him walk by my table. There's no proof."

"We have cameras at the shop," I stated. "Not great, but maybe we can find something to prove he took it. Then we'll go to the cops."

He sat down on the edge of the bed. "I'm not sure I want the cops involved," he said.

That gave me pause. Was he involved in something illegal. Was there a chance he was into shady business dealings? That made me stop and think about everything I knew about Ethan, which was almost nothing. I knew about his brother and the fact he didn't get along with his family, but that wasn't much. I didn't know what his business was. I didn't know if he was a part of the mob or something worse.

"I'm not asking for specifics, but is there a reason you don't want the police involved?" I asked softly. I moved to sit down beside him on the bed. "Is there something incriminating on that flash drive?"

"No," he said with a shake of his head.

"You're pretty desperate to get that drive back," I pointed out. "We're breaking the law. It seems like you've got something critical you want to hide."

"I'm not hiding anything," he said. "I'm the CEO of a company with stakeholders who count on me. There are documents about our financials on that drive. There is proprietary information about the company and the people who work for it. We have files on businesses we're involved in. It's just not something that should be published."

"I get it," I said. "But we should call the police. This guy might be trying to steal from your company. Could he work for the competition? I'm assuming you have competition."

"Possibly, but I'm more inclined to believe he's more interested in what dirt he might find on me and my family," he replied.

"What if he doesn't know who you are?" I said with hope. "It could all just be a freak thing. He might have been doing this to others. He might be a typical thief. A hacker looking for a way into your bank accounts and stuff."

He seemed to consider the possibility. "Maybe, but what are the odds? If he's been hanging out there for days, has he stolen from anyone else? Has anyone complained they had stuff go missing?"

"Not that I know of." I shrugged. "But he might not have had the opportunity. The shop was empty. You were in the bathroom. Cindy was busy. It could have been a crime of opportunity."

The more I thought about it, the more I had convinced myself that was exactly what had happened. I wanted that to be the truth. Something told me he was getting ready to run. The press was making his life miserable and he was going to flee. I didn't want him to leave. It was selfish, but I wanted him to stay a little longer. I was hoping we could talk and come to some kind of agreement about what this thing was between us.

"I have to find it," he said. "I don't know if it was random or targeted. I don't know if that guy connected you to me and is writing a story right now about you. About us. Have you seen him anywhere else?"

"I don't think so," I said. "I probably should have paid more attention."

He grabbed the laptop and opened it. As expected, there was a password on it. Ethan dropped it back on the bed. I could feel his frustration. I looked around the room. "He was only here for what, maybe five, ten minutes," I spoke my thoughts aloud.

I got up from the bed and walked to the door to replay what he might have done. There was the small table on one side. He would have probably put his key on the table. The desk in the corner would be where I would have sat down to work. If he stole the thumb drive, he would be anxious to see what was on it. I walked to the desk again and looked around. Then I smiled. I reached for the box of tissues and started pulling them out.

Sure enough, the drive was at the bottom. I pulled it out and held it up. Ethan had lifted the mattress and was searching. I whistled once. He popped his head up and looked at me. "Found it." I smiled.

"No way," he said with a laugh.

"Yep."

"Where was it?" He dropped the mattress back onto the bed and made it haphazardly.

"Tissue box," I said.

"Thank goodness," he breathed. "Let's get out of here."

I picked up the tissues and shoved them back into the box. A voice in the hall had us both stopping and looking at each other. "He's back," I whispered.

We were on the tenth floor. It wasn't like we could jump out the window.

"Fuck," he said. "I'll grab him, and you run."

"No!" I hissed. "Hide!"

"Where?" he scowled.

We didn't have time to argue. The door handle was turning. I rushed to the small closet and gestured for him to get in with me. He closed the door. We were plunged into darkness. The door opened and then closed with him talking loudly. I peered through the louvres on the door. It was just him. He was talking on the phone.

"I got it!" he exclaimed with excitement.

I could barely see Ethan's face. I didn't need to see his expression to feel his frustration. He was pissed enough to get violent with the man. I wouldn't blame him. I wanted to kick the guy's ass, too.

"I haven't looked at it yet, but I will now," he said.

I heard what sounded like him peeing. It was gross. Nasty. He was still talking on the phone.

"I'm going to look now," he said. "Yes, it was him. I know it was him."

I could only assume he was talking about Ethan. That pretty much cleared up that theory. The theft was intentional. It wasn't an accident or coincidence.

"Hold on," the reporter said. The toilet flushed and the reporter walked into the room. He was ten feet away from us. I wasn't sure what would happen if he caught us in the closet. Would he call the police? I doubted Ethan would give him the chance. He would kick his ass but that would no doubt bring the police into the situation.

"I'm going to go through the drive and finish my article," he said. "I'll send it to you tonight or tomorrow."

The man sat down at the table. He was settling in. It was only a matter of seconds before he went for the drive. He was going to discover it was gone. If he was alert, he was going to notice his stuff had been moved. We weren't exactly careful when we searched. My heart was pounding in my chest. We were about to get busted.

"It's a good story," the reporter said. "Trust me. This is big. I'm going to blow this thing wide open. I've got a twist to the story. No one else has it."

"You," Ethan breathed my name.

I nodded with understanding. I was about to get dragged into the story. I understood exactly what was happening. The tension was coming off Ethan in waves. Things were going to hit a breaking point. I wasn't sure how long we were supposed to wait in the closet.

We listened while barely breathing as the reporter walked around the room. He was pacing with nervous energy. He never specifically said Ethan's name when he talked about the story he was going to write. He didn't say my name, either. But it certainly seemed like we were the subjects of the story he was working.

Ethan's hand dropped to my hip. We were facing each other in the very small closet. I was afraid to move or breathe. Ethan's much larger body took up the bulk of the space. It was the exact wrong time, but it was happening. I was aroused. I was actually thinking about sex in a moment that was so not sexual. It was the close contact. The excitement. All of it. I wondered if he knew. Was he feeling it? Maybe it was just me. I hoped it was just me because I didn't think I had the willpower to tell him no if he tried any funny business.

I looked through the slats once again and saw the guy sitting on the edge of the bed. He was still on the phone, but whoever was on the other end was doing the bulk of the talking. I wondered what was being said. It was a little unnerving to think about total strangers talking about me. I understood why Ethan was not happy about them on his case.

"I'll talk to you later," the reporter said and ended the call.

The room was plunged into silence. I was afraid to breathe. How in the hell were we going to get ourselves out of the mess? Ethan and I stayed perfectly still. I was certain the guy sitting on the bed was going to hear my heart pounding in my chest. This was bad. We were in deep shit. The only way out was to confront the man. It was going to add fuel to his story. The plan might not have been the best. That was on me.

Chapter Twenty

Ethan

My dick was fucking hard. I had issues. I was trapped in a closet with what I would definitely call an enemy five feet away. It wasn't like I could fuck her in the closet. There was zero room and there was no way I could do anything without making noise.

When the TV came on, I exhaled. At least we could breathe without getting found out. Not that it mattered. Standing in the cramped closet until the guy left the room was not an option. We had to get the hell out. I was leaning toward just using brute force. There was no other option.

Ava put her finger to my lips and shook her head. She must have known I was about to make a move. She slowly moved, inch by inch, and put her back to the closet door. She pulled out her phone. The light felt like it was a spotlight. I quickly put my hand over the screen. She quickly tapped out a text and sent it.

I wasn't able to see what the text said. "Just wait," she whispered so low I barely heard her.

I nodded and waited. A moment later, the asshole's phone rang. "Hello," he answered. "Yes, this is he."

There was a silence for a moment. "Absolutely! I'd love to! I'll be there in five minutes!"

The guy put the phone down and rushed into the bathroom. "Yes!" I heard him exclaim.

The TV went off and a few seconds later, the door clicked shut. Neither of us moved for several seconds. "He's gone," she said. "Let's go."

"What's going on?" I asked.

She pushed open the closet. Fresh air washed over us. "Let's get out of here," she said.

"What's going on?" I repeated.

"Cindy called him," she said and rushed toward the door.

I followed her into the hall. I considered snatching the guy's laptop. If I was lucky, he wouldn't have his story backed up on a drive. If it was stored on the laptop, I could kill the story. In theory. Someone who made their living off of their files would have them backed up. But it would be nice just to be able to stick it to him a little. But stealing a laptop would make me the criminal. If he had LoJack on the damn thing, I would really blow up the story. He would still win.

"Is that who you texted?" I asked.

We were casually walking toward the elevator. The danger was over. We weren't going to get caught.

"Yes," she replied with a grin. "I think we make a pretty good team."

She pushed the button for the elevator. I grabbed her and laid a kiss on her. "I'm surprised by your criminal prowess."

She laughed and stepped back when the elevator doors opened. My smiled dropped. The reporter was standing in front of us. He looked at me, then Ava. I saw the moment he realized what was happening. He rushed off the elevator. "What the hell is going on?"

"Get out of my way," I growled.

"Oh, hell no," he said. "Were you in my room?"

"Get out of the way," I said again. "Get on the elevator," I said to Ava.

She stepped inside and held the door open for me. The asshole stood in front of me. "You're going to want to move," I told him in a low voice.

"Were you in my room?"

"Did you steal my thumb drive?" I shot back.

"Don't move," he said and shook his finger at me. "I'm calling security."

"Call the police," I said. "I want to file a report. You stole something from me."

He pulled out his phone and was going to make the call. I was fairly sure there were security cameras in the hallway. If he called security, they would look at the footage and see we had gone into the room. We could come up with a bullshit story and get out of it, but it would get her friend in trouble.

I stepped close to him and invaded his space. "Put the phone away," I said in a low voice. "You and I are even. If you want to make this a thing, I'm going to win. We've got the footage from the coffee shop. You stole something from me. I didn't take shit except for what was mine. Fuck with me and find out who I really am. Do you really think you're going to walk away from this without getting charges slapped against you? I will use my pull to bury you."

He shoved me hard. "Wrong move, asshole!"

"Ethan, let's go!" Ava ordered.

As if I was going to let the guy get away with it. I punched him. Once. That was all it took. He dropped to the floor wailing and holding his nose. "I'm going to sue you!"

"Get in line, asshole!"

I stepped into the elevator. The doors slid closed with him still hollering on the floor. "Fucker," I muttered under my breath.

"Are you okay?" Ava asked.

"I'm fine."

"You know he's going to call the cops," she said. "He's got a nice bloody nose to sell the story."

"It was worth it," I said. "If they want to push it, they will see he started it. He put hands on me. I defended myself."

"I know, but it's going to take time to sort it out," she said. "We have to get out of here."

The elevator stopped. Instead of going through the main lobby, we walked down the hall to a side exit. I pushed open the door and made sure there were no police around. I could hear a siren in the distance. I had no idea if they were coming for me or not, but I didn't want to stick around and find out.

"We'll go get my car," she said. "Are we safe at my apartment?"

"I don't know," I answered honestly.

We kept our heads down and walked to the coffee shop. There were a few more people in the place. My things were gone from the table. "I'll grab my stuff," Ava said.

I waited with my head down and the hat pulled low. Cindy and Ava returned. "I put all your stuff in the back," Cindy said.

"Thanks," I replied and took it back.

"Thank you for saving our asses," Ava said. "It was close."

"I'm glad I could help," she replied. "He never showed up, though."

"Uh, yeah, I don't know if he will," I said.

"Ethan knocked his ass out," Ava said.

Cindy looked shocked. "What?"

"He caught us leaving the room." I shrugged. "He got defensive and shoved me. I hit him."

Cindy started laughing. "Sounds reasonable to me."

"Me too." I nodded. "We should get out of here, though. And he might figure out you are involved."

"I'll deny it," Cindy said. "I'll play dumb. If he shows up, I'll ask why he didn't show up to meet me."

"Thank you," I said again. "I really appreciate the help."

"Me too," Ava said.

"I owe you," I told Cindy.

"Don't worry about it," she said, laughing. "This was the most excitement I've had in a year."

"Let's go," Ava said. "I don't want to stick around in case he comes back."

We walked to her car. I had my sunglasses on and kept my head down. She drove normally down the street.

"Are you feeling brave enough to swing by the store?" she asked. "If not, I can drop you off and go on my own."

"I'm good," I said. "I'll buy."

"You don't have to buy me." She giggled.

"What should we have for dinner tonight?" I asked. I was trying to return to normalcy. What had just happened was not normal. I would not be surprised if she asked me to leave her place.

"He knows," she said.

"Excuse me?" I asked.

"That reporter," she said. "He definitely knows now."

"Knows what?"

"About us," she said. "He caught us. What do you think happens now?"

I shook my head. "I don't know. I should probably think about leaving before this gets any worse."

"Nothing happened," she said. "We're fine."

"The guy is putting together an article," I replied. "He's going to publish it. We have no idea what he's going to write. He might have dug up dirt on you. You might be dragged through the mud."

"I have nothing to hide," she said. "Don't worry about me. Let's go get some food. We'll have a nice dinner and just relax. There's no reason we need to sit around and worry about what he might write. I know no one in my life is going to give him any information on me. He can put out whatever he wants, but the people who know me aren't going to be-lieve it. If they do, they aren't worth being in my life."

"That's easy to say now," I said. "But when your face and name are spread around with nasty rumors, it's hard. I've been through it more than once. I don't think you want to get mixed up in this. I'm sorry I've got you tangled up in my mess."

"Technically, it's your brother's mess," she said with a smile.

"I have to tell you something," I said.

"Uh-oh, that doesn't sound good," she stated.

"I was going to leave yesterday," I confessed.

"What?" She swerved the car when she turned to look at me.

"My friend back home told me stuff was heating up," I said. "I thought my best option was to get out of Hawaii in a hurry. He had somewhere for me to hide out in New York. I know I'm on borrowed time here. At least I was. Time's up. They found me. They found you."

"Were you going to say goodbye?" she asked quietly.

"Of course!" I answered and reached out to touch her hand. "Yes."

"Why didn't you leave?"

"The hurricane." I laughed. "My pilot said all planes were grounded."

She nodded and said nothing.

"You know I have to go back," I said. "This kind of thing is just going to keep happening. Hiding is doing nothing. Now I've not only dragged you into this situation, but your friend as well. Your boss. I never wanted to bring you into this. I hate that you're already involved."

"I understand you have to leave, but please let me know," she said. "If you sneak out like a thief in the night, I'm going to be pissed."

"I get it," I said. "I won't do that. I owe you that. If this guy presses charges against me, you have to let me take the hit. Do not try and defend me. I've got very expensive lawyers who will make this disappear. I'm not going to get charged. It's going to get muddy, but I can handle it. I don't want you getting dirty."

"I'm a big girl," she scoffed.

"I know, but this isn't your mess. You have been nothing but good to me. You've been incredible. I feel so fortunate to have you as my landlord. You saved my ass. You've helped me more than anyone else in my life. That means a lot to me."

"You sound like you're saying goodbye," she murmured.

"No, not yet," I replied. "I just really want you to know I'm sorry. I am going to find a way to pay you back. You deserve a million dollars."

She laughed at that. "Let's start with a fresh gallon of milk."

Chapter Twenty-One

Ava

I wasn't going to let his announcement bring me down. I knew he was going to be leaving soon. I just hoped he would say goodbye. It was going to be sad to see him go, but I understood why it had to happen. This was not his world.

"Lasagna?" I asked as I pushed the cart down the aisle.

"I could probably make that," he said.

"I can make it," I replied.

He tossed in a few things as we walked. Grocery shopping with him was an experience. He didn't stop and look at prices. He didn't look to see what the best value was. If he wanted it, he tossed it in the cart.

"If that's what you want, I could eat lasagna," he said. "It's been a while."

"Perfect," I said.

We picked out everything we needed for the dinner. He insisted on buying one of the cakes from the bakery. He even picked up some special treats for Roxy. As usual, he insisted on buying the groceries. The liquor store was next door. We bought a few bottles and finally headed for home. I was going to miss these very normal activities.

"What can I do to help?" he asked with a beer in hand. He leaned against the fridge and watched me.

I couldn't resist the urge to touch him. He looked so damn handsome. I rubbed my hand over his face. "I'm not sure it's a good idea for you to be in the kitchen," I said.

"Hey, I've been learning a lot the last couple of weeks," he said. He turned his face and kissed the palm of my hand.

"Yes, you have." I laughed. "Learning how the other half lives."

"When I do get home, I'm going to check out the kitchen in my place." He grinned. "I want to see what kind of dishes I have in that place."

I started laughing and went back to making the lasagna. "I can't believe you haven't been in your kitchen."

"I've been in the kitchen," he said. "I just haven't really used it."

"Same thing," I snarked.

"If you don't need me, I'm going to call Lucas," he said. "I need to give him a heads-up the shit is about to hit the fan."

"Go ahead," I replied with a smile. "I'll get this going."

He looked at me for a moment and I thought he was going to say something. Instead, he leaned down and gave me a soft kiss. "You're amazing," he whispered before walking away.

I was trying to stay busy to avoid thinking about what was coming. As crazy as he made me in the beginning, I was going to miss him when he was gone. My apartment was small, and while it was crowded, it was also cozy. It was nice to have someone to come home to. I liked being able to sit around and watch TV. I liked sharing dinner with someone and going for walks with my dog on the beach. I liked the companionship. I thought I liked being alone, but I was beginning to feel otherwise.

Being alone had been fine all these years. I thought I was satisfied with my life. I loved my freedom. But now, I was beginning to see the other side of the coin. It wasn't a loss of freedom. There would be some compromises, but they would be well worth it. I was tired of being alone. It was going to be so hard to go back to the way things were once he left. It was going to be a lot of retraining my heart and mind to be alone once again.

I could hear his low, masculine voice while he talked outside. I hoped he wasn't going to get into too much trouble for hitting the guy. If he needed a witness, I was more than happy to stand up for him. I hoped like hell the reporter left me alone.

Ethan came back into the kitchen. He pulled another beer from the fridge. "How did it go?" I asked.

He shook his head. "They aren't happy."

"They?"

"My friend Lucas, who also works for the company, did a three-way call with the PR team," he said.

"A PR team?"

"My company hired them to try and basically help wash the company's hands of my family's scandal," he said. "I'm supposed to be a good boy. I had to confess I punched the guy. They aren't happy."

I laughed and then stopped. "I'm sorry. It's not funny. I just can't imagine you getting scolded."

"Yeah, it didn't go well," he muttered. "They're reaching out to the magazine he writes for to threaten legal action for stealing the thumb drive. They're also going to look into stalking charges."

"Do you think it'll work?" I asked with surprise.

He shrugged. "I don't know. Maybe."

"Damn, you weren't joking when you said you've got lawyers on your side." I laughed.

"I told you, I will take care of this," he said. "I'm not going to let you suffer. I told my people to make sure the company knows this asshole has been stalking you. He's going to be told to stay away from the coffee shop. If you see him, call me. Take his picture. We're going to make sure he never comes back."

"My hero," I replied. I slid the lasagna into the oven. "Thirty minutes."

"Thirty minutes," he repeated with a sly smile. "That's more than enough time."

"For?" I asked with my own flirty smile.

He grabbed me, pushed me against the counter, and kissed me. I tasted the beer on his lips, which was so him. It made me hungry for more. I pulled at his shirt and he lifted his arms to help me pull it off, tossing it on the floor. He attacked my clothes, pulling them away and creating a pile on the floor. He bent his knees and sucked on my nipple with his hands cupping my breasts as I leaned back with my hands on the counter. He kissed over my breasts and then down my stomach. He dropped to his knees in front of me as his hands rubbed up my thighs, and then he reached up to grab my breasts. He buried his face against my stomach.

I reached for his head and held him against me. He moved his mouth lower and kissed above my pubic bone before burying his face against my crotch, his tongue lapping over my clit. I cried out and slapped my hand against the counter. He continued to kiss and suck at my clit while he slid his hands up and grabbed my ass, pulling me against his face and devouring my pussy. I was overloaded with pleasure. He was a master with his tongue, driving me wild until I couldn't stop the tidal wave of ecstasy. My body broke free, opening to him and then nearly collapsing on top of him.

He got to his feet and kissed me again and I tasted myself on his lips instead of the beer. He was savage. Primal. His hands were all over me and I struggled to keep up. I was still drunk on the lust he stirred inside me. In a flash, he flipped me around until I was facing the cabinet. His hands squeezed my ass and his mouth was on the back of my neck, his teeth sinking into the crook between my neck and shoulder.

He jerked my hips back and then pushed his hand on my back to bend me over. I felt his knuckles brush against the inside of my thigh. A moment later, I felt the tip of his cock brush over my swollen folds a second before he was pushing inside me with one hard thrust. His hard steel filled me, stretching and setting me on fire.

He thrust hard and bit down on my shoulder once again, and I cried out at the sensation overload. He released a sound that didn't sound human—he had never been so wild. He ravished me and was totally out of control. I loved it. He was a man who was always in control, except just then. Suddenly, he stopped moving.

"Ethan?" I gasped.

"Fuck."

"What's wrong?" I asked, alarmed.

"I... fuck, shit," he muttered. His forehead rested on my shoulder. "I'm sorry."

"Don't be sorry," I said. "It's good. Go. I'm good."

"I didn't put on a condom," he said.

That should have scared me more than it did. "I'm on the pill," I said. "I'm not worried about that. And I assume you aren't giving me anything."

"I'm clean," he said.

"Me too."

I heard him sigh. "Then we're good?" he asked.

"We're good," I answered. "We'll be a lot better if you get moving again."

He chuckled against my ear. "You might want to hold on for this."

I gripped the edge of the counter and held on for dear life while his body pummeled mine. The brief cool-off period was forgotten. The animalistic nature was back. It was like a switch flipped and he unleashed all his pent-up frustration. The adrenaline from earlier was fueling the crazed desire. When he thrusted again, it was over, both of us tumbling into sweet bliss. He leaned against me, wrapping one arm around my waist and kissing across my shoulder blade.

"Shit," he said. "Are you okay?"

"I'm good."

"Sorry if that was a little rough," he murmured and stepped away.

I slowly turned around to face him. "I think it was exactly what I needed. What we both needed. I get it. The adrenaline was still pumping through my veins after our little closet adventure."

He grinned and tossed some of my clothes at me. "I'm sure you felt my erection in the closet."

"I did," I said with a small laugh.

"I have no idea what that was about," he continued. "Kind of embarrassing."

"I was pretty aroused myself," I admitted.

"I think my dick knew," he said. "It picked up on the arousal."

I could smell the lasagna cooking. We both dressed again. "Dinner will be ready in about ten minutes," I told him.

"Can I do anything?" he asked.

"You can set the table," I replied.

It was a little strange to jump right back into making dinner after what we had just done. My body was still tingling. I slid the bread into the oven. That was one of the perks of being a part of a couple. Random sex in the kitchen while dinner cooked was definitely a perk. Sitting down to eat dinner with him brought me a sense of melancholy. I knew every dinner we shared was bringing us closer to the end of our time together.

After dinner, we took Roxy for our nightly walk. He held the leash with one hand and my hand with the other. We didn't talk much. I was certain he was feeling the same thing I was. We knew it was coming to an end. I invited him into my bed for the night. We held each other close and drifted to sleep together. I was so going to miss him. Sleeping alone was going to be something else I was going to have to get used to.

Chapter Twenty-Two

Ethan

I felt the moment she went to sleep. Her body relaxed and her breathing slowed. I tried to go to sleep, but I couldn't. My mind was spinning. I knew I had to leave. I didn't want to leave. I didn't want to leave her. I was looking for a solution. I wanted to find a way to keep her in my life. I knew that was impossible. I was still a Mitchell. I was the guy who ruined her family. No matter what we had between us, it wasn't going to be enough to overcome that situation. She might be able to forgive me for what happened with her family, but I doubted she was ever going to forgive me for not being honest with her from the very beginning. That was not cool. I screwed that up.

Getting to sleep should have been easy with her, but all the crap from my life was piling on. There was so much that needed to be dealt with. Nothing was going to get done with me in Hawaii. I needed to stop playing defense. It was time to go on the offense. I wasn't going to take it lying down.

When I woke the next morning, Ava was gone and I knew she was working. I got up with nothing immediate on my agenda. Before I checked my email to see how much trouble I was in for punching the reporter, I needed coffee. Ava had left a note on the counter.

Try not to punch anyone it read. *I have an early shift and then have to do a checkout checklist. I'll be home after lunch.*

I grabbed a banana and sat down to eat it. I was putting off the inevitable. I finished the first cup of coffee and then went to find my phone. Not surprising, there was a text from Lucas asking me to call him as soon as I was up. That was always a bad sign.

"Hit me," I said when he picked up. "What now?"

"I've got that pilot ready to go," he replied.

I wanted to tell him never mind. "For when?" I asked instead.

"How soon can you get to the airstrip?" he asked.

"I can't get there until later," I said. "Ava is at work."

"And?" he snarked.

"And I'm not just going to go while she's at work," I said a little defensively. "She deserves better than that."

"You're getting tangled up with her, aren't you?" he asked with a sigh.

"She's been good to me," I answered. "She's gone out of her way to help me out. I owe her more than just sneaking out while she's at work. That's not cool."

"I get it," he said. "But it's probably better if you get out of there now."

"What is your deal with her?" I asked. "You've been telling me to get away from her from the beginning."

I heard a door close. That concerned me. It sounded serious. I sat down on the couch, resting my hand on Roxy's side.

"She doesn't know who you are, does she?" he asked. "Is that still the going theory?"

"I don't think she knows," I replied. "If she did, I'm pretty sure she would throw me out on my ass."

"I think you're right there," he muttered. "Do you know the details about your brother's situation?" he asked.

"I know he got high with some people and one of them ended up dead," I said. "Right? What's there to know?"

"The woman he was with," he answered. "The lawyers say she's the one who brought the drugs to the party. She bought them. She scored.

If the drugs were bad, it's on her. If she's the one who gave the drugs to the kid who died, it's on her. Not Collin. Her."

"I get it," I said with a sigh. "It's going to be his defense. Her lawyers will say it was Collin. It'll be a he-said, she-said kind of situation."

"Yes, but I think we both know who's got more power and who will be believed," he said slowly.

"They are setting her up to be the fall guy," I said. "That's fucked up, but if she really did bring the drugs, then it's on her. I can't say I think either of them were in the right. They both deserve to pay if they gave that kid bad drugs."

"There's something else you need to know about the girl," he said.

"What?" I asked irritably.

"It's Ava's sister."

There was an echo in my head. I could hear a gong beating between my ears. I could not have possibly heard him correctly. "Who is Ava's sister?"

"The girl your brother was with that night," he said. "Her name is Jenny MacArthur. It's Ava's younger sister."

"Ava's last name is Hunt," I said.

"Ava uses her father's last name," he replied.

Bits and pieces were falling into place. She had told me her sister was involved with drugs. Her sister had reached out to her because she was in trouble. It couldn't be. There was no way. There was no universe that put her and I in this worst possible position.

"I think you're wrong," I said.

"I'm not. Collin's lawyers are working on a case that points the finger at Jenny. They are going to make her the fall guy. She's going to prison if this goes down the way it's projected to."

I shook my head. "No. No way. Tell them to find another legal strategy."

"That's not up to me," he said. "It's the best way to get Collin out of trouble."

"I don't care," I said. "He needs to fess up and take responsibility."

"How close is Ava with her sister?" he asked.

"They aren't," I replied. "That doesn't matter, though. Ava's the kind of person who will always put blood before anything else. She is never going to be okay with her sister being set up."

"We don't know that the drugs weren't hers," he said. "Collin says they are."

"Collin is a fucking addict!" I got off the couch and started to pace. "Why is anyone believing him?"

"I don't know that they actually believe him, but they do have to defend him to the best of their ability, and he's given them a solid defense," he explained.

"It's bullshit," I hissed.

"There's more," he said.

"Fuck me. How much more can there be?"

"Ava's family," he continued. "They hate you because you're the one who initiated a hostile takeover."

"I did?" I asked, aghast and horrified. "Are you sure?"

"Yes," he answered. "I pulled up the files. It was definitely you. It was one of your first really big moves. You saw a company on the brink of ruin. You moved in like a shark. It was you who dealt the final blow to the family business. They lost everything."

"Fuck," I groaned. "Why in the hell does it have to be the one person I find that I actually like?"

"There are millions of other women," he suggested.

"I'm sure I fucked over their family one way or another."

"I doubt that," he said. "This was a fluke."

"Do you know she works three jobs to cover the cost of her father's end-of-life care? "She begged her family for money to help her take care of him in his last days. I think part of the reason she couldn't get the money was because they didn't have any. Do you know why they didn't have any? Me. I fucking bankrupted them! I'm the one who made her financial situation so much worse."

"You didn't take her money," he said. "Her grandfather's mismanagement and shady dealings caused him to go bankrupt. He's the one who did that to his family. He ran that company into the ground. Not you."

I stared at the picture of her father. If Ava would have been able to get the money from her family, what would his last days have been like? Where would she be right now? I felt like I had fucked up her entire life. And then I brought all of this into her life. I was an asshole.

"Well, shit," I muttered. "This just gets better and better. What about the reporter? Do I get to look forward to a shitty piece in the local gossip rag about me and Ava?"

"I'm not sure what's going on with that just yet," he replied. "The reporter claims you broke his nose."

"I doubt it, but I hope I did," I snapped. "He sure as hell deserves it."

"He's going to milk it," he warned.

"I'll have to write a big check," I said. "Big fucking deal."

"I'm not sure money is all he's after," Lucas cautioned. "The guy is looking to boost to his career."

"He doesn't have a story," I scoffed. "He never got the chance to look at the files. He has nothing. I haven't done shit. I'm boring. The only thing he has is a busted nose. That's not going to win him a Pulitzer."

"He couldn't care less about the money," he said. "He's going to want an exclusive."

"There's no story!" I gushed.

"I just told you what the story was."

"What?"

"It's not just about you and Collin anymore," he said. "The Ava element is a new twist. It adds excitement. It adds juice."

An icy shiver ran down my spine. "You have to be kidding me. You cannot let this guy do this, Lucas. You have to find a way to shut him down. He's an asshole. I'll break his nose for real if he prints one bullshit lie about Ava. I want him shut down. If he won't stop, buy the fucking publishing company!"

"I get it," he said. "You're worried she's going to find out."

"That's inevitable," I groaned. "I'm worried she's going to suffer for my mistakes. I'm not about to let her get dragged into this. It isn't right."

"I know, I know," he said with a sigh. "But now you know why you have to get out of there. Every minute you spend with her, you're risking exposure."

"I know. I'll call the pilot after she gets home."

"You can't tell her anything," he warned.

"I know."

"You want to come clean," he said. "I hear it in your voice. Don't. She could very easily turn around and go straight to the press. I don't know what all you've done or said, but that doesn't matter. A woman scorned will not hesitate to throw a dude under the bus."

"Ava wouldn't do that," I said.

"Wouldn't she?" he asked.

"I get it," I replied. "I'll call once I've nailed down some plans."

After ending the call, I mulled over my next move. The right thing to do would be to tell her the truth. I should tell her, but I knew telling her would completely sever our relationship. Being apart from her that week had been brutal. If I told her, she was going to rage at me. She was going to be furious and hurt. I wouldn't get a goodbye. She would throw me off the island herself if she could.

Not telling her was going to be just as bad. she was going to find out who I was. It was only a matter of time before she realized her sister and my brother are connected. If her sister ended up doing time that my brother should be doing, it was going to kill her. Ava didn't talk to her sister and they weren't close, but I had a strong feeling she would stand by her anyway.

When Ava found out I knew and didn't tell her, she was going to lose it. If I didn't get out of her house before she found out, it was going to be bad. Really bad. I supposed I was a coward in a way. I was trying to escape before I had to face the consequences of my choices. That's what kind of man I was.

Chapter Twenty-Three

Ava

I was so relieved to walk through the door of the condo and find it relatively clean. That's what a good renter did. It wouldn't take me long to sanitize and change the bedding. Then I could get home to Ethan. I wasn't sure what we would do, but I was looking forward to just hanging out with the guy.

I was just finishing up my cleaning, when I got a call from a number I didn't recognize. It was a New York number, which could be only one person. I thought about ignoring the call, but it wasn't going to make it go away.

"What?" I answered irritably.

"Ava," Jenny said.

"You called me," I said. "Where are you calling from?"

"It's one of those prepaid phones," she said. "I had to get one. My other phone is blowing up. They won't leave me alone."

"Who won't leave you alone?" I asked, alarmed.

"The police. Reporters. I don't know."

"The police?" I asked.

"The reporters are the worst," she sobbed. "I can't leave my apartment. Every time I turn around, they are there. They're taking my picture and writing the worst stuff about me. It's not true. I can't escape them. My face is everywhere. I don't know how to get away from this. He said he would help me and now he's gone!"

"Who's gone?" I asked.

"I know he's going to blame me," she wailed. "I'm totally alone. The friends I thought I had are gone. They all ditched me. They know I'm toxic right now. I can't afford a lawyer!"

"Slow down," I said. "What are you talking about?"

I heard her take in a shaky breath. "I can't tell you all the details," she said. "Not yet. It's bad, Ava. Really bad. I'm in such deep shit. I need help."

"I don't know how I can help you if you won't tell me what is going on," I said.

She coughed and dragged in a breath. "I can tell you it involved the Mitchells," she said. "They are determined to destroy our family."

"The Mitchells?" I asked with a burning low in my stomach.

"Yes," she replied. "They are going to ruin me. I'll never have the chance to do anything. They hate us. I should have known better. I'm so stupid!"

"Where are you?" I asked.

"I'm in a motel out of town," she answered. "I had to get out of there. They won't leave me alone. I can't get away from them!"

"Jenny, are you drunk? High?"

"No!" She started shrieking. "I took a couple of pills to calm down. I'm not high."

I rolled my eyes. I wasn't surprised. "I don't know what you want me to do," I said. "I'm in Hawaii. I don't have any money. You won't even tell me what's going on."

"I can't," she repeated. "I apparently signed some stupid paper that said I can't talk about anything or I can be sued."

"By who?"

"Them! The Mitchell family."

I shook my head and tried to make it make sense. I didn't understand why the family was out to get us. What had we done to them? It wasn't even us. It was our parents and grandparents. They were all dead and we were still being forced to pay the price. Whatever happened had to go way back. I just wanted them to go away. They had to leave us alone. We deserved to live in peace.

"Jenny, I want to help you, but I don't know what I can do," I said calmly.

"I just need you," she murmured. "I need my big sister. You are the only person I have left in the world. You are my sister. You're my only family."

She was killing me. Tugging at my heartstrings and making this so much worse. I wanted to be there for her, but she was fucking toxic. She would pull me into her shit. I couldn't save her five years ago, I couldn't save her now. She was still using. Still making some horrible choices. How was I supposed to help her?

"I don't know what to say," I said. "I think you need help, but I certainly don't have the means to help you. Can you at least tell me why the police are after you?"

"Someone died and they are going to blame me," she wailed.

My stomach dropped. "Did you have anything to do with it?" I asked with my tongue sticking to the roof of my mouth.

"No. I mean, maybe. I don't know."

That was all I needed to hear. "I have to go," I said.

"Ava, wait!"

I hung up. I told myself a long time ago I had to practice some tough love. She wasn't going to stop doing what she was doing if she was always getting bailed out. She was just like Ethan's brother. Jenny had been coddled her whole life. My mother didn't parent her. She was her friend. The two of them were great friends. They partied together and shopped together. They did everything together. Mom died and Jenny was spiraling. I just didn't know how to help her.

It broke my heart to think of Jenny in prison or dead. I didn't want it to happen, but I couldn't stop it. She was going to hit bottom whether I was there or not. Showing up out of nowhere in her life again would not end well for me. I was going to be associated with her poisonous ways. I didn't want to risk losing myself to save her.

I drove home with my mind elsewhere. When I walked through the door, Ethan was just walking out of the shower. I looked at him and his beautiful body. It almost made me cry. I was going to lose him soon.

"What's wrong?" he asked and walked directly to me. "Ava?"

I didn't realize it, but tears were running down my face. He pulled me into his arms and held me. "What happened?" he asked.

I sobbed several minutes before pulling back. "I'm so embarrassed," I said.

"Don't be." He smiled and pushed my hair out of my face. "Let me get you some water."

He went to the fridge and pulled a bottle out. He was thoughtful enough to twist the cap before handing it to me. "Thank you."

"You're welcome. Do you want to talk about it?"

"It's nothing," I shook my head. "I just, well, it's my sister."

He stiffened and pulled back. "Your sister? Is she okay?"

"No," I answered. "She's not."

"What happened?"

"I'm not sure," I replied. "She wouldn't tell me details. She said she couldn't tell me details because she signed some paper. It sounds bad enough that she might end up in jail. Or prison. She's into the drugs again. Not that she ever stopped. She says she's being set up to take the fall for something that she may or may not have been a part of. She won't tell me what's going on but wants me to help her. I don't know how I can help her if I don't know. I'm all the way over here and she's there. She knows just what to say to make me feel like shit."

"I'm sorry," he said.

"She made me feel guilty for not saving her," I went on. "Pulled the sister card. We haven't been sisters in a long time. I know she is only saying it because she's desperate."

"What do you want to do?" he asked softly.

"I want her to be well," I said. "I want her to stop making such horrible decisions. All the things I want to do are impossible to do. Everyone always says you can't help someone who doesn't want to be helped. It's true. Jenny is only asking for help now because there is a real chance she might have to pay a steep price for her shitty decisions."

"What kind of trouble is she in?" he asked.

"I don't know," I said. "She did say it involved the Mitchell family."

He choked on his water. "What?"

"I swear they have it out for us," I said. "I don't understand why. What did I do to make them hate me? That's a rhetorical question because I know I didn't do a damn thing. They are evil, vindictive people with no souls. My grandfather pissed them off and now they are coming after me and Jenny. Who does that? What kind of assholes do that shit?"

"I don't know," he said and looked down at his feet.

"Jenny said the press is hounding her," I continued. "It's like we are living the same life but different. I'm worried about the press hounding me and she's gone into hiding. She called me from one of those burner phones. I think she's hiding from the police. I think it's only a matter of time before the police call me. Do I tell them I've talked to her? Am I harboring a fugitive?"

"She's not in your house, so you couldn't be accused of that," he replied. "But if the police do contact you, be honest. Tell them what you know. You don't know anything, right?"

"No." I shook my head. "Not really. I know she's hiding somewhere. She won't tell me what she did. She won't tell me what it was that happened. I don't know anything."

"Exactly," he said, nodding. "That's all you have to tell them. You don't know anything. They can't drag you into this. Tell them you haven't talked to her in a long time. Do not let them buffalo you into saying or doing anything."

He was acting kind of strange. He seemed like he knew a little too much about dealing with the law. What kind of man was he? Then I remembered his brother gave him the same kind of trouble my sister was giving me. This was his way of life. And he had ended up running away from all of it to end up here. He was going to leave. I was his escape. All of this was just a reprieve in his life.

"I'm..." I stopped and gave myself a head shake. "I'm going to go for a drive."

"A drive?" he asked.

"Yes." I nodded.

"I'll come with you," he offered.

"No," I said. "I need to be alone. I need some time to think. I'll be back later."

"Are you sure you're okay?" he asked with concern.

"I'm fine," I said. "I just need some space. Roxy, come. Let's go bye-bye."

I walked out of the apartment. I didn't stop to think. I just put the dog in the car and took off. There was a spot I liked to go to when life was really getting me down. My mind was burdened with thoughts of my childhood. I thought about my little sister when we had been so close. I missed her. I missed that life. I missed the simplicity of knowing I was going to wake up in the morning to my mom making breakfast and my dad rushing off to work. I missed the good old days.

I stopped at the stop sign for a half second before hitting the gas. I heard screeching tires. I turned to look to my right just in time to see a car barreling toward me. I barely had time to even think of what to do. I felt the impact and for the briefest split second, then I felt excruciating pain. Then, there was nothing.

Chapter Twenty-Four

Ethan

I paced the small apartment. Something didn't feel right. She'd been so upset when she left. At first, I thought maybe she knew of my family's involvement. If she did, she wouldn't have allowed me to hold her. I didn't think she knew. She was just reacting to bad news. I was glad I was there to comfort her, but I wondered what happened next.

The guilt I felt was immense. My family was orchestrating the destruction of her sister's life. Ava would never recover from the guilt she felt not knowing how to save her sister. When it all came out and she realized I had sat idly by and let it happen, it would destroy her. I knew she let few people into her life. When all this went down, she would never trust another person. The guilt was chewing a hole through my stomach.

I checked the time again. It had been two hours. I tried calling her, only to realize her phone was sitting on the table. She had left without it. I had a feeling that was intentional. She didn't want to be disturbed. I certainly knew that feeling. I had come to Hawaii with the same intention. I often turned off my phone and ignored it as much as possible.

I looked out the window. It was getting dark. She had exposed me to some of her favorite places on the island. They were all remote. If something happened, how was anyone going to find her? She wouldn't be able to call for help. She was on her own. I told myself not to worry. She'd been taking care of herself long before I showed up. She knew the places well. I knew she liked to get up early to see the sunrise and enjoyed the sunset just as much.

I shouldn't worry. She was fine. She and Roxy were just doing what they did. I thought about making myself a drink to help the time pass by. I wanted to stay sober for when she got back. She would need me. I wasn't sure what I was going to say. It felt like a total lie to continue to comfort her when I knew I was very much responsible for her misery.

It was weird, but I kind of missed the dog. I wasn't used to being in the apartment by myself. It felt a lot bigger with no one else in it. I had craved silence and isolation. I got it now. Now, I craved company. I wanted my adopted family.

Ava's phone rang on the table. It was wrong to answer it, but something told me it was important. "Hello?"

"Hi," a woman said. "I'm calling about the dog. It says her name is Roxy."

Something didn't feel right. "Roxy?" I asked. "What about her?"

"I have her here," she said. "The poor thing looks terrified. A nice couple brought her in about an hour ago."

"Brought her where?" I asked.

"To the shelter," she said. "They thought she might be from that accident."

"Accident?" I asked with confusion. "I'm sorry, you have Roxy?"

"Yes, this is the number on the dog's tag. Is this Roxy's owner?"

"Roxy was with her owner," I said, growing more worried by the second. "What accident?"

"There was a car accident," she explained. "The people who found the dog thought she might have been the one the police were looking for."

I couldn't make sense of it all. "Okay, I know I sound ridiculous, but I'm confused. Was Ava in an accident?"

"I believe so, but I don't know the details," she answered. "The police notified the shelter there was a missing dog. After the accident, the dog took off. The police tried to catch her, but she ran. The couple found her and brought her here. She had some blood on her, but we've looked her over and she doesn't appear injured. My guess it was from the young woman in the car."

I was going to puke. "Ava was in an accident," I breathed.

"We'd love to get Roxy home, but if she needs to stay overnight, we can do that," she said. "Are you the husband?"

"I'm..." I stopped. "Yes," I answered. "Tell me your address. I'll come and get Roxy."

She gave me the name and address of the shelter. I wasn't going to panic. I took a moment to collect myself before ordering an Uber. Then I called the first hospital that came up on my search. It took some convincing, but I was finally told she was in the hospital. First the dog, then the woman. They didn't want to tell me anything over the phone, but in person it would be a different story. I knew how to get my way when I was looking at someone in the eyes.

I got to the shelter and asked for Roxy. The woman behind the counter brought her up front.

"Roxy." I dropped down to greet her. "How are you, girl? Are you okay?"

The dog licked my face. "Do I need to do anything?" I asked.

"We just need you to sign the papers saying you picked her up," the woman answered.

"She's not hurt?" I asked.

"She seems fine," she replied. "There was a little blood on her, but we washed it off. Our vet tech looked her over. She's good."

"Thank you again," I said. "Let's go home, girl."

The Uber driver wasn't exactly thrilled to have the dog in the car. I gave him a very big tip. "Don't go anywhere," I told the driver once he delivered us back to the apartment. "I need a ride to the hospital. Just give me a minute to get her settled."

"Okay," he agreed.

I took Roxy in, made sure she had water, and food and promised her I would be right back. The ride to the hospital was intense. Now that I knew Roxy was safe and secure, I couldn't stop thinking about Ava. She had to be okay. I refused to accept any other reality.

"Excuse me," I said to the woman behind the glass in the emergency room.

"Can I help you?"

"I'm looking for Ava Hunt," I replied.

"And you are?"

"I'm—" A little lie wasn't the worst thing in the world. "Her husband."

The woman looked me up and down. She didn't believe me, but was she really going to ask me for ID? I doubted it. If she wanted to challenge me, I was up for it. I would happily accept that challenge. It had been nearly an hour since I got the call. Almost three hours since the accident happened. My stress and patience were reaching a breaking point. I didn't want to be that guy, but I would absolutely threaten to buy the hospital and fire everyone if they didn't let me see her.

"Let me check," she said.

I waited while she tapped on some keys. "Looks like she's just back from X-Ray. They are getting her a room for the night."

"What?" I asked. "Why? What's wrong?"

"You'll have to talk to the doctor about that," she replied.

"Fine, where is the doctor?"

"One second and I'll have someone take you back," she said.

I was on the verge of pulling my hair out. I paced back and forth. Her idea of one second was very different than mine. I was about to pound on the glass when a door opened. "Mr. Hunt?"

I was assuming she was talking to me. "Here," I said. "I'm Mr. Ava Hunt."

It was the most ridiculous thing I ever heard. "Follow me," the woman said.

She hustled down a corridor, stopped, and pulled back a curtain. Ava was lying in a bed and she was out. "Where's the doctor?" I asked.

"He'll be in as soon as he can," she said. "We just had a trauma come in."

"Is she, uh, is she asleep?"

The nurse offered a small smile. "She's in and out," she answered. "You can talk to her."

"Thank you," I said.

I moved to the side of the bed and stared down at the woman I had developed some serious feelings for. I was afraid to touch her. I didn't know what was injured on her. She looked hurt all over. There was still blood in her hair and on her cheek. The left side of her face was puffy. A cut on the side of her head was stitched closed. There was dried blood in the corner of her mouth and in the crease of her neck. Her left arm was wrapped from her fingers to just above her elbow.

I gulped down the lump in my throat. She didn't look good. I needed to know what happened. Panic was bubbling up and threatening to take over. She looked like she was going to be okay, but was she? What was happening on the inside? Did she have brain damage?

The noises on the other side of the curtain got louder. Whatever was happening over there didn't sound good. I assumed it was the trauma the nurse referred to. I moved to the other side of the bed and very gently took Ava's hand in mind. I brushed my thumb over the back of it. An IV was in her arm. The machine monitoring her heart and blood pressure beeped once. She stirred and I thought she might wake up.

"I'm here," I said gently. "I'm right here."

I had no idea if she could hear me. I just wanted her to know I was there for her, whatever that meant. I reached up and brushed a strand of hair from her face. She was pale and looked so small in the bed. I wanted to kiss her and make it all better. How in the hell was I supposed to walk away from the woman? Just thinking about losing her had nearly sent me into a tailspin. I was so grateful she was okay. At least, I hoped she was okay.

"Ava, Roxy's home," I said. "She's okay. I know you're sleeping, but I bet you're worried about your girl. She's okay. She misses you."

She moaned and moved her hand, but her eyes never opened. My heart hurt seeing her suffering. I leaned down and gave her the lightest kiss on her forehead.

"Excuse me?"

I popped my head up to see a uniformed police officer. "Yes?"

He looked at Ava and grimaced. "Poor thing," he said. "How's she doing?"

"I don't know," I said. "I just got here, and the doctor hasn't been in yet. What happened?"

"She got T-boned," he said.

"T-boned?" I asked.

He nodded. "I was coming by to let her know she was in the clear."

"Why wouldn't she be?"

"We weren't sure what happened," he said. "I talked with the witnesses. Miss Hunt had the right of way. The other driver blew through the stop sign and slammed into her."

My anger spiked. "Did you arrest him?"

"Oh, he's arrested." He nodded. "He was wasted. The witnesses said he didn't even touch the brakes. Did they find the dog? I tried to catch her, but that poor thing was scared."

"I got her," I said. "She's home."

"Are you the boyfriend?" he asked.

"I'm, uh…" I wasn't sure what to say.

The man smiled. "It's okay. I know Ava. She works at my favorite coffee shop. I know she's not married. Your secret is safe with me." He pulled a business card from his pocket. "Give this to her when she wakes up. I'll have the case information. She'll need it for her insurance."

"Is the guy in jail?" I asked.

"He will be," he said. "He's being treated and then we'll book him."

"I hope you throw the book at him," I growled.

He nodded once and walked out of the room. I was tempted to go find the guy and beat the shit out of him. How dare he hit my woman. I touched her shoulder. I made myself stop touching her. I had no idea where she was hurt. My gentle caresses might actually be causing her pain.

I didn't know how long I waited before the doctor finally showed up. He was staring down at the iPad in his hand. He looked up and seemed startled to see me. "Hello."

"Hello," I replied. "What's wrong with her?" I asked.

"You are?"

"Her husband," I answered sternly.

He knew I wasn't, but he was not about to argue with me. "Ava has sustained a concussion, but I don't see any brain injuries. She broke her left arm, but lucky for her, she doesn't need surgery. She's bruised and is going to be very sore for the next week or so."

"What about her head?" I asked. "Are those the only stitches?"

"She's got stitches in her arm. All in all, she's very lucky. She'll heal, but she needs rest. We're keeping her tonight because of the loss of consciousness. As long as nothing develops overnight, she'll be released tomorrow."

Relief washed over me. "Thank you."

"A nurse will be in shortly to move her upstairs."

"What about the sleeping?" I asked.

"It's normal," he said. "We'll keep an eye on her all night."

I nodded and took her hand again. She was going to be okay.

Chapter Twenty-Five

Ava

Pain. I was blinded by it for several seconds. Everything hurt. I tried to open my eyes. My eyelids hurt. I tried again. They opened a sliver. Bright light slashed at my eyes. It felt like a million knives were stabbing into my skull. I could hear faint beeping from somewhere far away. I opened my eyes a little wider. There was more brightness.

"Ow," I groaned.

I looked around the unfamiliar surroundings. "What the hell?" I murmured.

I tried to raise my left hand. It felt like there was a brick on it. And damn did it hurt. I looked down and saw it was wrapped in a gauze bandage. I lifted my other hand and discovered I was connected to an IV. I was groggy as hell. It felt like I was trapped in a dream. Everything hurt, but I also felt like I was floating.

I was in the hospital. Why? Why was in the hospital and why in the hell did my body hurt so badly? I tried to remember. Thinking hurt my head. The door opened and the noise that had been faint was suddenly very loud. Ethan walked in carrying a cup of coffee.

"Ethan?" I asked with confusion.

"Hey." He smiled. "You're awake."

"I am. I think. What is going on?"

He closed the door and came to stand beside me. "How are you feeling?"

"Awful," I croaked. My throat hurt.

"Hold on, let me get you some twater," he said.

He rushed to pour me a glass from the pitcher. He held it for me while I took a sip. It hurt to drink. "My head is killing me," I said.

"I bet." He nodded. "You took quite the hit."

"Is my arm broken?" I asked.

"It is," he replied. "You have a concussion. Or a had a concussion. I'm not sure how that works. You've got some stitches on the side of your head and pretty much every inch of you is bruised. Severely bruised."

My head was still muddled. "I don't understand."

"You were in a car accident," he said gently. "The police said a guy blew through a stop sign and slammed into you on the driver's side."

There was a flash. A memory. I jerked when I felt the impact all over again. "Roxy!"

I remembered someone calling for the dog. They kept saying 'get the dog.' "Where's Roxy?" I started to tear up. I would never be able to move forward if she was dead.

"She's home," he said and touched my cheek. He wiped away a tear. "She's perfectly fine. She's okay. Someone picked her up and took her to the shelter. I picked her up and took her home. I haven't been back but I'm sure she's fine. I made sure she had food and water."

"You haven't been back?" I asked.

It felt like I was drunk but sober. Like being underwater with heavy shoes. He grabbed a chair and pulled it over to sit next to the bed. "Not yet."

"What time is it?"

"Eight," he replied.

"In the morning?" I asked. "Is it the next day? I'm really confused."

"The doctor said you might be confused," he answered. "They aren't going to let you go until they know there isn't a brain injury. It's the next morning."

"I hurt," I said. "I don't think I've ever felt this much pain."

"I'll get a nurse. They've got you on some pain meds, but they didn't want to give you too much."

"No, not yet," I said. "My head is really foggy. I can't think straight."

"You don't need to think straight," he replied with a smile. "You just need to rest and heal. Your body needs it."

"But Roxy is okay?"

"Roxy is perfect," he assured me.

"What about my car?" I asked.

He shook his head. "I have no idea. A cop did come by and left his business card. He said you'll need to call him to get the case information for your insurance."

I groaned. "Oh no. I don't have that great of insurance. This is going to cost me a fortune."

"No, it's not," he said.

"I'm in the hospital. That isn't cheap."

"I'm taking care of it," he replied.

"No," I shot back, and then winced. "No way."

"Yes," he retorted. "This hospital stay is going to cost you more than it would have because I'm a spoiled jerk."

"What are you talking about?"

"They were going to put you in a room with someone else," he said. "They told me I wasn't allowed to stay because visiting hours were over. Needless to say, you're in a private room and I can stay as long as I damn well please."

I tried to smile but it hurt. "Ow."

"Just get some rest," he said. "I'm glad you're awake, but I want you to get some rest."

"I want to go home," I whined.

"I think you need to wait and let a doctor decide that," he said. "Let me get a nurse to get you some pain meds. Are you hungry?"

"No. I don't think so. My throat hurts."

"Let me get you some water."

He helped me with the water and then went out to find a nurse. The doctor came in shortly afterward, and after a few questions, he decided I needed to stay another night. I wanted nothing more than to go home.

After the doctor and nurse left, Ethan took my hand in his. "Are you okay?"

"I want to go home," I sobbed.

"I know," he said softly. "This is better. If the doctor wants to keep an eye on you, you need to stay. A head injury is no joke."

It hurt to cry. It hurt to talk. It hurt to breathe. "Will you tell Roxy I love her, and I'll be home soon?"

"I will," he replied with a smile. "Your pain meds are going to kick in soon. I'm going to go home and check on Roxy. I'll be back in an hour, two tops."

"My car," I murmured half out of it.

"What about it?"

"I need to call my insurance."

"I'll take care of it," he said. "You rest. Sleep. Do not move."

I couldn't if I wanted to. He kissed me again and then stayed with me until I fell asleep. When I woke again, it was a nurse standing next to my bed. "Hi," she said with a smile. "How are you feeling?"

"Like crap," I murmured. "What time is it?"

"It's after lunch," she said. "You were asleep. Your husband said he would make sure you ate something, but he wanted you to sleep."

"My husband?" I asked.

She smiled. "Shh," she whispered. "We know he's not your husband, but he certainly acts like it. You're a lucky girl. You need to lock that man down. He is crazy about you."

"Ethan?" I asked with confusion.

"Yes, Ethan. He just stepped out to make a phone call. He'll be back in soon. That man has not left your side for more than ten minutes at a time."

"Really?"

"I was on the floor when you were brought up last night," she said as she worked. "He about lost his mind when we told him he couldn't stay. He woke up the administrator, and thirty minutes later we were putting you in this room. It's the VIP suite."

"It is?"

"Oh, yes, honey," she replied. "Your man treats you good."

I smiled at the thought. "I know."

Ethan came in just then. He frowned at the nurse. "Did you wake her?"

"No," I quickly answered. "It wasn't her."

"Told you," the nurse sang. "Make sure she tries to eat something," she ordered Ethan.

"I will," he replied and took his seat next to the bed again. "How are you feeling after that nap?" he asked.

"I wish I could say better, but my head is still pounding," I said. "I'm afraid to know what I look like."

"You're beautiful."

"You're a liar," I said with a small laugh. "Do you have a mirror?"

"I don't think you want to see a mirror," he warned.

I groaned. "That bad?"

"You're just a little banged up," he assured me. "You're going to heal. The doctor said the bruising was going to be bad today and a little worse tomorrow, but you're healing. The bruises will fade."

I touched my cheek. "I don't want to sound vain, but can I please have a mirror?"

"Sit tight," he said.

He went into the bathroom and returned a moment later with a small shaving mirror. He held it against his chest. "Are you sure?"

"Yes," I said. "I need to know what I'm working with."

"Just remember you're going to heal," he said.

He held the mirror up for me. "Oh, my goodness!" I touched my eye. "Holy shit!"

He pulled the mirror away. "It's going to fade."

"I look like I've been in a fight with Tyson!"

"Why don't I show you a picture of your car," he said. "Once you get a look at that, you'll think your face looks pretty damn good. It could have been so much worse."

"You have pictures of my car?"

"I had to go by and get the insurance stuff out of the car," he said. "I didn't want to go snooping through your drawers and stuff. I figured it would be easier to just get the insurance card. I saw it there when I was putting the extra napkins in the glovebox."

"Okay," I said. "Let's see it."

He leaned down and showed me the pictures from his phone. "Wow," I murmured. "It's destroyed."

"When I saw the car, I couldn't believe it," he said. "If I would have seen the car before I saw you, I probably would have lost my shit."

"And Roxy is okay?"

"Roxy is fine," he said. "I was going to go back to the apartment and walk her. I'll be back with dinner. You have to eat."

"I don't think I'm hungry."

"If you don't eat, you don't get out of this place," he said.

"Fine, but I've never been a fan of the cafeteria food," I said. "I avoided it when my dad was in and out of these places."

"I will bring you a cheeseburger," he said. "Good?"

"Very good. Thank you."

He gave me a quick kiss before walking out of the room. I watched him leave and thought about how amazing he was. He was the kind of man who would take care of me. I supposed I wanted that. I liked my independence, but it was so nice to know he was going to take care of things for me. I did need to rest. I could only do that because he was there to handle things and take care of Roxy.

I drifted back to sleep feeling completely at ease despite my pain.

Chapter Twenty-Six

Ethan

"Come on, girl," I said to Roxy.

She walked inside with no enthusiasm. "I know," I said. "I'm going to go get her right now. We'll be back in a few hours. You've been such a good girl. I'm going to get your mom and you can snuggle with her all day because we are not letting her out of bed."

I rubbed the dog's head and removed the leash. I had come back to the apartment bright and early in the morning to let Roxy out and to shower and change clothes. I knew it was silly for me to stay the night at the hospital, but I couldn't bring myself to leave Ava. She'd been so pitiful. The nurses had their hands full. I didn't want her to wake up and need something. I wanted to make sure someone was there to help her if she needed it.

"Hopefully, we'll be back soon," I said.

I grabbed the keys for the rental car and left the apartment again. The nosy neighbor was standing out front, glaring at me while she watered her plants. "I'm calling the landlord," she said.

"You do that."

"Did Ava move out?" she asked.

I didn't answer her.

"I'm telling the landlord you're staying at the apartment," she said.

"You said that already. Good luck with the rest of your day."

I got in the car and sped away. When I got to the hospital, the nurse was in the room. I carried in the bag of clothes she requested. "Good morning." I smiled.

"Good morning," she replied.

"Is the doctor coming around soon?" I asked.

"He'll be by soon," she said.

"I brought you a change of clothes." I held up the bag.

"You're a good boyfriend," the nurse said with a big smile. "When my husband and I were first dating, he was good to me."

I didn't correct her. I put the bag in the chair and helped fluff the pillow behind Ava's head.

"The doctor will be around soon," the nurse said before walking out of the room.

"Everyone keeps calling you my boyfriend or husband," she commented. "I think they see something we don't."

"I had to tell them we were a couple," I explained. "They weren't going to let me stay if I didn't. We have to keep up the ruse until we get out of here."

"I get it," she said. "But is it really a ruse?"

"What?"

"You've been at my side day and night since this happened," she said. "I just don't think we have to pretend this is nothing when it's very much something."

I smiled and nodded. I wasn't sure what to say to that. I wanted to say yes. She was obviously thinking about a relationship. She wanted it. I wanted it. But I couldn't. I could not have a relationship with her unless I came clean. If she still wanted me after that, maybe then we could have the relationship she was talking about.

But I couldn't. She was looking at me, waiting for me to say something. I had to say something quickly before more time passed and it got awkward. I didn't want her to feel weird. Inside, I was thrilled she had even mentioned it.

Thankfully, the door opened, and the doctor came in. "Doctor's here," I said.

I stayed out of the way while the doctor did his thing. "I think you're good to go," the doctor said. "But I would feel better if you had someone to help you for the first few days."

"I'll be there," I said.

Ava smiled at me. "Thank you."

"I'll send a nurse in with instructions," the doctor said.

"Do you need help getting dressed?" I asked her.

"I think I can manage," she replied.

"I'll help you to the bathroom," I offered.

I handled her like she was made of the most fragile glass. She was weak, and despite her claiming to be okay, I could see she was struggling to stand. "Lean on me," I whispered.

"I'm sorry," she murmured. "I thought I was better."

"You're healing," I said. "Just hold onto me."

I bent down to pull her panties up her bruised legs. I had brought a pair of black sweats and a loose shirt with a light jacket. I carefully dressed her. "I brought a jacket, but I've just realized it's not going to go over your cast."

"I'll be okay," she said. "Thank you so much. I'm a little embarrassed."

I grinned and kissed her nose. "It's not like I haven't seen it all before."

"True. That's a little comforting."

"Come on, let's get you back to bed," I told her.

We shuffled across the room. I helped her into bed and then gently put on her socks and shoes. "I feel so helpless." She sighed.

"You're weak today. We'll get you home and I know a certain canine who is looking very much forward to snuggling with you. You'll feel better tomorrow."

"Thank you so much for being here," she said. "I honestly don't know what I would have done without you."

"Your dad's friend, Richard, I think was his name, he would be here," I said. "You've got people who are worried about you."

"Richard has never seen me naked." She laughed. "I definitely wouldn't want him to dress me."

"Good point," I said. "Are you hungry?"

"I am, but I'll wait until I get home." I could tell getting dressed had exhausted her. She had paled again.

"Close your eyes," I said. "You know these things can take a while."

"I'm just going to close my eyes," she murmured.

I sat down to wait. What the hell was I doing? I should have been running in the opposite direction. Last night I had watched her sleep and tried to imagine my life without her in it. I couldn't leave. I didn't want to leave her. That hour or two when I had no idea what was happening with her, I had been having one of those moments. It was like my life was flashing before my eyes, but instead of my past, I was getting a glimpse of my future. There were two roads. One was with her and one was without. The road without her had been dark and dreary.

In that dark hour, I didn't know if I had a choice. But we were through the darkest part. I did have a choice. I knew what I wanted. I just wasn't sure how to make it work. Last night had brought me some clarity. I knew I loved her. I couldn't pinpoint the moment I fell in love, but when the possibility of her not coming back to me happened, I realized I loved her.

I reached up and stroked my hand over one of the bruises on her unbroken arm. Every bruise was a testament to how close I had come to losing her. I didn't tell her about the very visceral reaction I had when I saw her car. I had nearly collapsed. The entire driver's side of her car was in the passenger seat. There was blood on the passenger seat. Her blood.

"Are you okay?" she murmured.

"I am. I should be asking you that."

"You've been asking me that," she reminded me.

I got up and touched her face. "I'm so glad you're okay," I said. "I can't tell you how worried I have been. You gave me quite a scare."

"Sorry. I didn't mean to."

"I know." I nodded. "I'm so glad you're okay. I know you're not okay yet, but you will be. I'm going to make sure of it."

I leaned down and gave her a quick kiss. "I love you," I whispered against her lips.

I didn't even know why I said it. It just came out. She smiled and held my face. She didn't say it back, but that was okay. I didn't expect it. Before she could say anything, a nurse came into the room with a wheelchair.

"All right, lovebirds," she said. "Load up."

I picked her up and gently placed her in the wheelchair. She reached for my hand. "My hero."

"I'm just returning the favor."

I grabbed her things and slung the bag over my shoulder. I retrieved the flowers from around the room and followed behind the nurse who pushed Ava in the chair. I was so glad to be taking her home.

Chapter Twenty-Seven

Ava

Despite being in total pain, I had never been happier. He loved me. I couldn't believe it. He loved me. I was so damn happy. I wanted to say it back to him, but he stunned me speechless. I had hoped he had feelings for me. I would have never guessed he loved me. I wanted to sit with the feeling for a couple of minutes.

"I parked the car in one of the designated spots," Ethan said. "I'll go get it."

The doors slid open and it was like walking into a stadium as the headlining band. I blinked as flashes went off in my face. Ethan immediately stepped in front of me. People were shouting Ethan's name and mine. They were asking all kinds of questions. None of it was making sense to me.

"Get her back inside," Ethan shouted to the nurse.

The nurse pulled my chair back. Ethan walked backward and did his best to shield me with his body. I didn't think it was going to do much good. The photographers were everywhere. The flashes continued to go off. The doors slid shut only to open again with a couple of very bold photographers following us into the waiting room.

"Get out of here," Ethan barked. "Get security over here!"

"Whoa, honey," the nurse said and whipped the chair around to face me in the opposite direction. "I didn't realize you were famous."

"Me either," I said. "I don't think I am."

She was pushing me down a hallway with Ethan behind us barking orders at the hospital staff and threatening the photographers who got close. The nurse pushed me into an open room. Ethan walked in behind us.

"Shit," he cursed. "Dammit."

"What is going on?" I asked him.

"We need to get out of here," he said. "Can you keep her here while I talk to security?"

"Make it fast," the nurse said.

Ethan walked out of the room leaving me with more questions than answers. "Is that normal?" I asked the nurse.

She snorted. "I had some hotshot singer in here a few weeks ago," she said. "That happened when I took him out the front door. I didn't know you were a celebrity."

"I'm not." I sighed. "My boyfriend is. Well, he isn't. Not willingly. He doesn't want to be a celebrity, but there are some pretty nosy press people who won't leave him alone."

"Is he a movie star?" she asked.

"No. He's just got a brother who's a troublemaker. But they were saying my name, weren't they?"

"They were saying all kinds of things," she answered. "I didn't understand most of it."

Ethan returned. "We're going out the back. I've got security bringing the rental car around. I can take her from here."

"Sorry, it doesn't work that way," the nurse said. "I have to get her to the car, or I get in trouble."

I felt like a fugitive being pushed through the back halls lined with empty beds and carts. Ethan was walking fast, looking more pissed by the second. I knew my head was foggy, but none of it was making sense. How did they know I was in the hospital? Why were they calling my name when it was Ethan they were after?

"Right here," Ethan said. "Keep her out of the doorway. I want to make sure it's clear."

I loved when he was bossy, and all take charge. "Clear," he called back.

The nurse pushed me outside to what looked like a delivery entrance. Ethan picked me up from the chair and put me in the front seat. "Thanks," he said and waved off the security guard.

He hopped into the driver's seat and punched the gas. He sped away from the hospital. Once he put some distance between the hospital and us, he slowed down.

"Ethan, what was that?" I asked.

"The same thing it always is," he muttered.

"But how did they know?" I pushed.

"Know what?"

"How did they know you were going to be at the hospital?" I asked. "And why were they calling out my name? Did they ask me how long we'd been together?"

"I don't know," he said. "They were asking a lot of things. I was ignoring them."

"Did something happen in New York?" I asked.

"I don't know."

He was being curt. His answers were short. Something was off. "Ethan, what is going on?" I asked.

"It's fine," he replied. "I'll get it under control."

"What are you getting under control?" I asked.

"Nothing."

"Ethan!" I shouted. "What the hell is going on?"

"I don't think we can stay at your place," he said.

"What are you talking about?" I asked again. My head hurt but now it was throbbing.

"I'll explain everything," he said. "Let's get you home and into bed."

"I thought we couldn't go to my place?"

He blew out a breath. "I don't know where else to go right this minute."

"Roxy," I said. "We have to get Roxy."

He drove to my apartment, but as expected, there were a bunch of photographers hanging around out front. "Shit," he cursed. "I knew this was going to fucking happen."

"What do we do?" I asked.

He drove around the block. "I'm going to leave you here. I'll jump the fence and get Roxy. I'll bring her back."

"Roxy can't jump the fence," I said.

"She'll be fine," he insisted. "Stay in the car. If someone comes by, just keep the door locked."

"Be careful," I said. "I'm going to call Cindy. She has a spare bedroom. Maybe she'll let us crash at her place for the night."

"Do that," he said and hopped out of the car.

I watched him disappear into the alley. I called Cindy. "Hey, I've got a problem," I said when she answered.

"Are you okay?" she asked with concern.

"Yes, I, uh, well, I need somewhere to crash for the night," I said. "Me and Ethan. And Roxy."

"Of course," she said. "What's going on?"

"That reporter from the shop the other day must have called his friends," I said. "There was a mob outside the hospital and now there's a mob outside my apartment."

"No!"

"Yes," I said. "Ethan is jumping fences and going to rescue Roxy."

"I'm so sorry," she said. "Come over. I was on my way out, but you know where the key is."

"Thank you," I said.

"I'm sorry you're having to deal with this when you're still injured," she said. "What assholes."

"I agree."

I ended the call and waited for Ethan to return with my dog. It was the craziest thing I had ever dealt with. Part of me was still wondering if it was all in my head. I had a brain injury. The whole thing could be a hallucination. Maybe I was dreaming. I wanted to believe none of it was real, but I felt pain. I didn't think anyone felt pain when they were dreaming.

I heard a bark and turned to see Roxy running toward the car with Ethan right behind her. He opened the back door. She hopped in and immediately tried to get into the front seat with me. She was making happy noises and licking my face and arm. Ethan got into the car and started to drive.

"Don't let her hurt you," he said.

"I'm fine," I said while trying to dodge a dog tongue to my lips. "I missed you, too, girl. I am so happy you're okay."

"I think she's saying the same thing." He chuckled.

"I called Cindy. She said we could go to her house. She has an extra bedroom."

"Tell me where to go," he instructed.

I quickly gave him the address. "Ethan, when we get there, you need to tell me what's going on. Something has changed. I want to know."

"I promise, I'll tell you everything," he said. "I have to."

He sounded upset about it. Once we got to Cindy's house, he insisted on carrying me in. I felt perfectly capable of walking. "Where is the bedroom?"

"Down the hall to the right," I directed.

He carried me to the bed and gently laid me down. He spent a long time fluffing the pillows behind me and pulling the blanket over me. I loved how he fussed over me, but I had a feeling it was more about him trying to avoid telling me what was going on. He was trying to protect me. It was endearing but annoying. Roxy hopped onto the bed beside me and curled up in a ball.

"I'm going to order you some dinner," he said. "You need to eat."

"Ethan."

"Let me order you some dinner," he said. "You have to eat so you can take the pain meds. The doctor was very specific about this. You have to stay ahead of the pain."

"Just order a sandwich," I muttered. "And then we have to talk."

"I know," he replied. "Don't move. I'm going to order the food. Roxy, take care of our girl."

He rushed out of the room. Something told me things were about to get messy. I dreaded it but I had to know. We could work through it. He loved me. We could figure out the rest.

I rubbed Roxy's head. "I sure did miss you, girl," I murmured. "I'm sorry you were scared. I never meant for you to get hurt."

She rubbed her head against my leg. "We're going to stay here for a day," I told her. "I promise, I'm going to get better soon. Then we'll get back home."

I closed my eyes and leaned back. My life was taking quite the turn. Everything felt out of place. With the way things were heating up, I had a feeling it was going to drive Ethan away. He was worried about this exact thing happening and it was. The man was too good. He wouldn't want me to suffer because of his brother. I had a feeling he was going to protect me by leaving me. That was going to gut me.

Chapter Twenty-Eight

Ethan

I was stalling. The moment I told her the truth she was going to kick me out. I wasn't sure I would get to see her again. The timing sucked. She was in no condition to hear the truth, but there was no hiding it. A rapid-fire exchange of texts between me and Lucas told me what I suspected. The story had broken wide open. Ava was officially involved. She needed to know the truth.

I accepted the food delivery that included water and soda. I had put in another order for dog food and all of Ava's favorite snacks. I wanted her to feel at home. It was my fault she wasn't able to recover in her own bed. I carried the food back into the bedroom, tossing a cheeseburger to Roxy.

"Thank you," she said and took a bite of her burger. "This is good."

I sat on the foot of the bed and tried to eat my own, but it was like eating a shoe. "I'm going to grab your pills," I said and got up.

"You need to tell me," she said quietly. "You're putting it off. There's no time like the present."

I sat down again and took a deep breath. "My name is Ethan Mitchell," I said. "My brother is Collin Mitchell. My parents are Robert and Marie Mitchell."

She nodded. "Okay."

"Ava, I'm the CEO of Mitchell Industries."

She squinted and appeared to be thinking. I saw her putting it together. "I don't understand."

"I'm the CEO of the company that took over your family's company," I said. "So, to answer the question that's on your tongue, yes, I'm one of those Mitchells."

"Oh," she murmured. "I see."

"I know that pisses you off, but there is more," I said.

"Great," she muttered and tossed the cheeseburger into the bag.

"My brother Collin is, well, you know what he is," I said. "That's all that true. My brother was at a party with drugs. I don't really know what drugs, but there were a lot of them. One of his friends took the same drugs. He overdosed and died."

She nodded. "You told me that."

"What I didn't tell you, and what I just learned a couple of days ago, is the woman with my brother at this party was your sister. I didn't put it together because of the different last names. I was just told. I swear I had no idea it was your sister with my brother that night."

Her eyes narrowed. "Your brother is the one setting my sister up."

"I don't know anything about that," I said. "My brother was or might still be trying to make a run for congress. The people running his campaign are looking for the best way to minimize the damage to Collin's career."

"By blaming it on my sister," she said.

"I don't even know what to say," I replied. "I honestly don't know. When I first found out Collin was involved in something sketchy, I decided to leave. I didn't know the details. I didn't want to know the details. I purposely avoided knowing too much. I knew he'd been partying, which was pretty normal. I heard about the guy who was killed. My brother of course said it wasn't him. He says he didn't know anything. When I left New York, Collin was still claiming innocence. The big question was whether or not he had been at the house when the guy overdosed. The lawyers are hoping to say the guy overdosed after he and Collin parted ways."

"Does it make a difference?" she asked.

"No," I answered. "Not to me or you. The lawyers are looking for a way to get Collin out of it. They'll admit he had a relapse and got caught up with the wrong crowd. He went home and the guy died."

"You mean my sister was the wrong crowd," she said.

It was shameful, but I nodded. "I think that's what they are going to try and sell."

"That's what she said," she murmured. "I didn't believe her. I don't even know if she's okay. Do you know? Did you know? I came home and told you about my sister. You stood there and listened to me talk about her. You knew!"

"I didn't. I found out that morning. I was going to talk to you about it when you got home. I knew I had to tell you, but I was so afraid of what you would say. I know how much you hate my family. I didn't know about your sister. I swear."

"Does that really matter?" she asked. "You were lying to me about everything else. That's why you're here. Did you pick my house to get to me?"

"No!" I said with a shake of my head. "I had no idea who you were. I didn't know about our family connection. I left New York to get away from that bullshit. I planned on working from here. I didn't want to be a part of the cleanup crew for Collin's latest mess. I just wanted to run away from all of it. I figured they would do what they always did. They would send Collin away for a month and let things die down. But that's not going to happen this time. The scandal broke wide open. There are charges pending and it's just a hot mess."

She stared at me with disbelief. "You thought I knew who you were. You thought I took your laptop and exposed who you were. You knew how I felt about your family and thought I would stoop low enough to sell you out."

"I did." I nodded. "I had just found out there was information leaked to the press. I couldn't find my laptop and I knew how you felt about the family. I figured you put it together or maybe you knew already, and it was your way of getting back at me."

"I would never do that," she said.

"I know you wouldn't," I said softly. "I know you would never do that. I knew it then, but I was spinning out. When the press showed up at my house that day, I knew it was getting bad. I didn't want to involve you. I was going to leave days ago because I didn't want them to find out our connection. I swear to you, I wanted to protect you. Now that they have figured out where I've been and who you are, the scandal is even bigger."

"I don't understand why you didn't just tell me all of this earlier." She sounded hurt.

"Because you would have kicked me out of your life," I replied honestly.

"Why do they care about you and me?" she asked.

"Ava, you and I are the older brother and sister of the two people caught up in a huge scandal," I said. "This is the twist everyone loves to read about. It's juicy and gritty. You are a part of the scandal just like I'm part of my brother's scandal. You changed your last name, but reporters like that prick who was in the coffee shop, are relentless."

She put a hand over her mouth. "What the hell?" She gasped. "Me. They're after me."

I slowly nodded. "I'm sorry."

"Holy shit," she continued. "They know Jenny is my sister. I'm with you."

"I'm so sorry," I repeated. "This is so unfair to you. I wish I could somehow take it back. You don't deserve this."

"Why didn't you tell me?" she groaned. "How am I supposed to deal with this? My sister. Your family is going to destroy her. You destroyed my grandfather and now you're going after my sister. You people are evil. How dare you! Was I part of this? Were you trying to set me up in some way?"

"Ava, no!" I moved to take her hand. She pulled it away from me. "I would never do that to you. I didn't know then. I got to know you and I couldn't stop myself from falling for you. I swear to you, I wanted to leave to spare you. I didn't want you to be involved."

"Too late," she sneered.

"I know." I nodded in shame. "I know I should have told you sooner. Lucas told me to stay away from you. He warned me this would happen. I didn't want to lose you."

"Why didn't you just leave?" she asked.

"Because I wanted you," I said.

She shook her head. "You wanted me to fuck you."

"Ava, no," I came back quickly.

"You should have left," she said.

"I know I should have. I'm a coward. I didn't want to go back to New York and face the music with my family. I got it in my head I could have it all. I was managing the company from here with Lucas's help. I was getting to spend time with you and see this beautiful place. I liked my life here. I liked being with you. I was hoping to find a way to tell you who I was and beg you to forgive me with my next breath."

"I don't know what to believe," she said. "I don't know what's real and what's manipulation."

"I never manipulated you," I defended. "Never. I didn't try to hide who I was."

"Except you did," she said.

"What happened with your grandfather and the company was not a malicious act," I said. "It was business. I know it doesn't make it better, but it was nothing personal. I didn't know your family. I didn't target them because of who they were. That's just what the company does. We buy up companies that are struggling. I didn't come here knowing who you were. It was nothing like that. When you first told me how much you hated the Mitchells, I wasn't worried. I didn't think this thing between us was going to go anywhere. Then it did. I developed real feelings for you."

"I don't know what to do with that," she replied. "You lied to me. I don't think I believe it when you say you developed feelings. I can't trust you."

"Please forgive me," I begged. "I swear to you, it's all real. My feelings are true. None of it was fake. I've been struggling to leave Hawaii because I didn't want to leave you. The night of the storm, I thought I was going to leave. But I couldn't, Ava. I couldn't leave you."

She wiped a tear from her cheek. "Even if your feelings are real, I don't see how that matters. Look what you and your family are plotting against my sister. You have the power of your name and your wealth behind you and you are using it to convict a woman who can't stand up to your family. Don't say you're not doing it, because you are. You know what they are doing and you're letting it happen."

"I'm not letting anything happen," I said. "I don't know the truth about what happened that night. I've never asked."

"You're suggesting it's okay to put my sister in prison for something she may or may not have done as long as your brother gets to walk away free and clear," she snapped. "Your family steamrolls over anyone that gets in the way of what they want."

"I am not my family. You know me, Ava. I've spent more time with you than I have with them in all my thirty-seven years. You know me. You know what I feel for you is real. I could never fake something like this."

"That's what you say," she murmured and furiously wiped her wet, bruised face.

"When I got that call about Roxy that night, my world stopped. There were a couple of hours when I didn't know if you were going to survive. I thought I was going to lose you. I realized I loved you that night. I will give up everything for you. But—"

She rolled her eyes. "Of course."

"The company is a sinking ship right now," I continued. "I don't care about me or what happens to my brother. I do care about the hundreds of people who work for us. They're going to lose their jobs. I have to do something to help them. I don't know what that is, but I can't just let it happen."

"So, Jenny taking the fall is a small sacrifice for the good of your company?" she scoffed.

"Definitely not," I said honestly.

She shook her head. "I don't know what to say. You've shocked me. You let me think you were someone else. You let me fall for a man who doesn't exist."

"I do exist," I insisted. "I'm right here. I'm real. Everything I've told you is the truth."

"You say that now, but what happens tomorrow when you remember another truth? How much am I supposed to take?"

Please, Ava, I know this is bad, but please, please forgive me."

THE END

TOUCH THE SEA BOOK THREE
Dancing
on waves
bestselling author
a u t u m n   g a z e

Touch the Sea Series

Book 1 – Seduction Island
Book 2 – Gentle Rhythm
Book 3 – Dancing on Waves
Book 4 – Stormy Waters
Book 5 – Tempting the Ocean

Find Autumn Gaze:

Autumn Gaze Newsletter:
https://www.autumngaze.com/sign-up
Autumn Gaze Facebook Page:
https://www.facebook.com/AutumnGazeAuthor
Autumn Gaze Website:
http://www.autumngaze.com

Want to read more...

FREE BOOKS?

Sign up for Autumn's newsletter
And she'll send you updates on new releases, ARC copies of books
and a whole lotta fun!
Sign up for news and updates!
https://www.autumngaze.com/sign-up[1]

---

1. https://l.facebook.com/l.php?u=https%3A%2F%2Fwww.autumngaze.com%2Fsign-up%3Ffb-clid%3DIwAR19Pln3ibiSJ3sbPjqwZi2C2ouEk0HNj3WPfqfFHOACbgTxP-nyPseA8z2I&h=AT2zXnGSz1iKPMdJCv3D1jaSfPpsk9GF78_lcDB8lQuthwcLpds-du_0dX1lpDVC_R_aw9eie2R8y7wQzGrIpKgoi-6TEh8H8t1IcDKGEJ-NzgaLtedWWgkAd-PDYhWUrxkU

More by Autumn Gaze

Department of Defense

Dead Ahead
Blue Falcon
Joint Service
Indirect Attack
Book Trailer:
https://lumen5.com/user/lexy-timms/dead-ahead-trailer-l12dn/[1]

---

1. https://l.facebook.com/l.php?u=https%3A%2F%2Flumen5.com%2Fuser%2Flexy-timms%2Fdead-ahead-trailer-l12dn%2F%3Ffbclid%3DIwAR0LhBM3pT9aIz8DEG5FXeXsDrBzasZgjxKC6RXAoj-yP8niyxJHcfLGE_o&h=AT2jwhb69pufcA2B8U84he2HH7eSLXUodpU-gOLs5q6X6DES914B03gx4E9QEWM8qS9YJJpajWAAa9yWDp1Ha2ExKlr1ICtVEhiTQ1NRqL-gY6naiPq1OCugPceon3NwSkXZM

Wicked Fates Series

Book 1 – Beautiful Darkness
Book 2 – Twisted Darkness
Book 3 – Wicked Darkness

Don't miss out!

Visit the website below and you can sign up to receive emails whenever Autumn Gaze publishes a new book. There's no charge and no obligation.

https://books2read.com/r/B-A-RKRU-POKDC

BOOKS2READ

Connecting independent readers to independent writers.

Did you love *Gentle Rhythm*? Then you should read *Dead Ahead*[2] by Lexy Timms and Autumn Gaze!

The only easy day was yesterday...

<u>Tri:</u>

I'm a Navy SEAL on a mission to find out what's happening in a politically-charged environment. When things go horribly wrong, I find myself saddled with my exact opposite: a female scientist who never runs out of questions or words. Now we're stuck on a deserted island with no way off and information vital to avoiding World War III. Will we make it off the island in time to warn the world what's coming? And will we do it with our hearts still intact?

<u>Ashley:</u>

---

2. https://books2read.com/u/bOzByo

3. https://books2read.com/u/bOzByo

They sent me to an island to find out why the marine life off the coast was behaving strangely. The only problem? It's a contested land inhabited by terrorists. When I find myself stranded on the island with a Navy SEAL who saved my life, I don't know whether we'll make it off alive. But one thing I do know? I might be falling for the man with the haunting blue eyes. Before we find out whether we have a future together, we have to escape terrorists, get off the island, and save the world.

Department of Defense Series:

Dead AheadBlue FalconJoint ServiceIndirect Attack

Also by Autumn Gaze

Department of Defense Series
Dead Ahead
Blue Falcon
Joint Service
Indirect Attack

Touch the Sea Series
Seduction Island
Gentle Rhythm

Wicked Fates Series
Beautiful Darkness
Twisted Darkness
Wicked Darkness

Watch for more at www.autumngaze.com.

About the Author

Autumn Gaze writes stories about love and life. She grew up reading every book she could get her hands on and still loves reading and watching movies. Stay tuned for more news to come!

She is joining USA Today Bestselling Author, Lexy Timms, on a few collaborated series and can't wait to share the Department of Defense Contemporary romance series with readers!

Read more at www.autumngaze.com.